Mistakes Made

B. Heather Mantler

Mantler Publishing Prince George

Library and Archives Canada Cataloguing in Publication

Mantler, B. Heather, 1987-, author
Mistakes made / B. Heather Mantler.

ISBN 978-1-927507-13-1 (pbk.)

I. Title.

PS8626.A676M57 2014 C813'.6 C2014-901212-8

To the members of Scribblers Unanimous, the regular, intermittent, and the seldom. Unanimous, not anonymous, because we don't want to stop writing.

HERTHA HEARS MORE THAN SHE SHOULD HAVE AND FINDS SOMETHING SHE LIKES.

"What do you want!" Proster's anger caused his face to go red and the muscles to stand out. Hertha flinched at the amount of rage in his voice and posture. Rarely had she seen her father display such emotion and all over a guard entering the room. Proster had been sitting on the edge of the dais in the throne room talking to his wife, Ruana, when the guard had entered.

Hertha knew the guard had been wrong to enter without knocking, but Proster usually tolerated it and would maybe give the guard a dressing down. Today somehow things were different, but they had been different since Narda, Hertha's sister, had disappeared two weeks ago. Hertha had sat up here at her listening post every day to find out what had happened, but her father had been so busy he had not talked about it with anyone. Hertha knew her parents had not talked about it because her mother had a worried expression on her face when she thought no one was looking.

The guard stood a good foot taller than Proster and yet it did not look that way. The guard had been with Proster a long time and did not flinch at the anger. Instead he placed the scroll he was delivering on the floor, apologized for interrupting, and withdrew from the throne room. Proster stood a moment longer before deflating back to sitting on the dais, this time with his head in his hands.

Ruana had not been fazed at all by the outburst as she stood there in front of the dais. She had just stood there and waited for it to be over. When Proster had sat back down, she had sat down beside him and wrapped her arms around him. They sat without speaking.

Hertha leaned forward, but her listening post had some large disadvantages. Back when the castle had been built someone decided to build a hallway ending high on the wall of the throne room. It was a significant drop down to the floor and Hertha was fully aware that if she fell, it would likely kill her. Why anyone would put in such a thing was beyond Hertha, but then again this castle had a back door that was similar. Her father had told stories of coming in the back door when he attacked the castle and captured it. The back door was usually locked, but the alcove above the throne room merely had a tapestry over it. Hertha could sit up there and not be seen while listening to everything said below. She just had to be careful of getting too close to the edge.

The words coming from below were soft and Hertha had to strain to hear them. Her father's voice, which had always been strong and youthful, was trembling and sad. Hertha struggled to keep herself together as she listened even before she really understood the words.

"Narda went through the portal," Proster said, "She and her friend from the marketplace went after the children when they saw the demon take Lord Vila's son. They managed to rescue the children, but Narda ended up removing the portal guardian from his post and taking his place. She cannot come home and never will be able to."

Hertha knew her father loved all three of his children equally, but Narda had been his favourite. No one had been bothered by that, except maybe Ruana when Narda got away with certain things. Hertha had her own life and Zebulon was too busy in his own head to pay attention to much else.

"I wish she had stayed home," Proster said, "I wish she had let the rest of us find the children and bring them home. But she did what she thought she had to do and she took responsibility when it was necessary. She said she was going to close the portal to make sure nothing more would come through and bother us."

Proster did not say anything more and Ruana just sat silently holding on to him. Hertha sat there without moving, or making a sound. It was quiet for several minutes.

"What should we tell people?" Ruana asked.

"I do not know," Proster answered, "I do not want to tell them anything, but people will want to know what happened to her."

"We do not have to tell them anything," Ruana said, "We just say it is a private matter and none of their business. That is the truth and they do not need to know anything else."

"Thank you," Proster said.

"She is alive and she has done her best to keep us safe," Ruana said, "It will be all right."

They were silent again. Several minutes went by before Proster gathered himself together.

"I guess I should see what message they left for me," Proster said before getting up and going across the room to the scroll. He picked it up and brought it back to sit down again. He unrolled it and read it to himself.

"What is it?" Ruana asked when he had finished.

"Grankle is sending a Lord Pardes to see if a trade agreement can be reached," Proster answered, "He will be lucky if I do not toss him out on his backside just for being in the wrong kingdom." Proster rolled the scroll back up and set it on the dais.

"As long as what you are doing is what is right for this kingdom," Ruana said.

"There are many times when I am not completely sure what exactly is best for this kingdom," Proster said, "But this is not one of them. The Kingdom of Proster is fine without any trade agreements. We have all the food, resources, and money we need and a good enough army to stop anyone from taking it. The only thing I question right now is whether it needs a different king."

"Do not give up," Ruana said, "Right now you are the king it needs and there are no others available for the position."

"I know," Proster's answer was somewhat muffled. They sat in silence again.

Hertha, figuring she had heard everything of

importance for the moment, slowly and quietly slid back away from the edge. Once she was far enough away, she got to her feet and headed down the hallway.

Hertha went to her room, where she changed her clothing. She removed the princess dress of blue satin and beaded decorations. She dressed in a brown skirt, beige shirt, and light brown wrap. She pulled her hair out of the high and fancy style that her maid had put in this morning, quickly making a basic braided bun with loose strands. When she was ready, Hertha slipped through the hallways to the door near the kitchen which led out to the court yard. Once in the court yard she did not need to hide or sneak because there were so many other people there no one asked any questions.

Outside the side gate of the court yard, Hertha found her friend Darwin waiting for her. He was leaning up against the wall with his hands in his pockets. His blondish hair was tousled, his blue eyes focused on something not visible to her, and his small nose was slightly sunburnt. He was skinny, long, and always hungry. Hertha had gotten her height from her mother, or Darwin would have towered over her instead of just being a head taller. His clothes looked similar to hers, but his were dirty with kitchen waste and stuff from the stable. His life was doing odds jobs around the castle.

They had met when he had brought firewood up to her room back when she was six. She had talked to him then and which was more than anyone else had done, so they became instantly friends. He had been seven at the time. Now they would sneak out and go to the market place a few times a week. They usually were not missed and if they were it was easy to come up with some story.

"What took you so long?" Darwin asked when he finally noticed Hertha.

"I was listening to the news," Hertha answered as they started toward the market place.

"Anything good?" Darwin asked.

"Not really," Hertha answered, "Grankle is just sending some nobleman to try and get a trade agreement out of my father."

"And how many times have they tried this?" Darwin asked.

"Probably once for every seventeen years I have been alive," Hertha answered, "Most of them have found themselves out of their rear ends."

"I have never figured out why they keep trying," Darwin said, "Or what your father's problem with Grankle is."

"My father came from Grankle," Hertha said, "And as he tells it, his father was starving him and his men because he did not feel the need to pay his army. My father and his men packed up and invaded this kingdom. When they had conquered it and divided up the spoils, his father showed up to claim the whole kingdom. My father kicked him out and swore repercussions if he showed his face around here again. From then on relations were tense, but Grankle does not want to let go of relations. Currently they are in need food, money, and resources, which we have."

"That explains the trade agreements," Darwin said, "Why does your father not invade Grankle and put it out of its misery?"

"I think he likes to watch them wallow in their own misery," Hertha answered, "Especially since he claims they created all of their own problems and have not figured out how to solve them without help. His father is no longer king, but the current king is arrogant and ignorant. Overall, I do not expect this person to stay any longer than the last one."

They reached the market place and started to wander. Darwin and Hertha looked at various stalls. Their discussion focused on the things they were looking at. Hertha paid for something for each of them to eat.

They were half way through the market when there was a yell farther down. The whole crowd parted for a group riding through. There were six or seven riders all together and all with the same nobility symbol on various pieces of clothing. The lead rider was blond haired, blue eyed, tall, medium build, and expensive clothes. He was not bad looking, but Hertha would not have though him handsome. However, the man riding behind him caught her eye. The man had brown hair hanging passed his ears, brown eyes, and a slightly bigger build than the first man. His high cheek bones and soft lines of his face made him easy for Hertha to watch. Her eyes stayed on him until he was passed and she would have to turn her head to continue to watch him. She did not pay attention as the rest of the party went by, but Darwin did.

"It looks like the nobleman from Grankle has arrived," Darwin said.

"He looks like an arrogant jerk," Hertha replied.

"Relax," Darwin said, "It is not like you have to marry him. He will be gone within the day if the previous ones are any indication."

"Let us go see if we can find some of that really good bread," Hertha said.

"It was down here somewhere," Darwin said taking Hertha's arm and directing her down the street.

A couple hours later Hertha and Darwin headed back to the castle. At the kitchen door, Darwin left Hertha there to go do chores he had put off. Hertha went inside. She went around the kitchen to the hallway beyond. In the hallway, she came across the brown-haired man from the group which had come into the city earlier. She watched him out of the corner of her eye as they passed each other. Hertha looked over her shoulder at the man and found he was looking over his shoulder at her. He smiled and winked. She smiled back. Then she had to turn back around and headed up to her room.

Hertha changed back to her princess dress and redid her hair in the fancy style. She put her market place clothes on the shelf under her bed. Hertha adjusted the bedding so it was difficult to see she had moved them. Then she left her room.

Hertha headed back up to her listening post above the throne room. Her father was sitting on his throne with Garrick and Herwin standing in front of him. They were busy conferring. Hertha sat down near the edge and held the tapestry far enough out so she could see without anyone below noticing.

"Those are the current cases from the lower court in need your attention," Herwin said. Proster nodded without any other sign he heard what was said.

"Proster," Garrick said loudly. Proster slowly looked up at Garrick as if Garrick over-stepped his place, not as if his attention was brought back to the present.

"All those cases are things you two should have the ability and experience to deal with," Proster said,

"None of them need my attention because none of them are unique or controversial. And I have plenty of other things I need to do without wasting my time with the work I have delegated to you two. I have told you both not to press your beliefs on to me."

"You have not been focused on things that are necessary for this kingdom," Garrick said, "You are still king and are needed here."

"I have heard every word both of you have said to me about the business of this kingdom," Proster said, "And I have given you my thoughts on what needs to be done. They have been the same responses I have always given for the same problems you always bring to me."

"In most things, yes," Garrick said.

"We are wondering why you are letting Lord Pardes stay here," Herwin said, "Especially as you have thrown out all other dignitaries from Grankle."

"I do not know exactly why," Proster answered, "I was ready to kick him out, his presentation was not persuasive, and I have no plans to sign any agreements with Grankle. Grankle can burn and I will only order the border to be wet to avoid the fire spreading. But my gut told me to let Lord Pardes stay and I cannot explain it. When I can, or when I find out why, I will explain it to you two. One or both of you can sit in on any sessions with him if it would make you feel better, but I will not be giving any thought to trade agreements with Grankle. Also I have given orders for a guard will be with them at all times and discussion on military weaknesses are to be avoided."

"I will sit in on those sessions," Garrick said, "I will remain silent during them. But there are other things that suggest your attention is not on running your kingdom."

"I have other things on my mind," Proster replied, "But those are private matters and are not up for discussion here. My kingdom has enough of my concentration for things not fall apart before those matters are settled."

"And how long will that be?" Garrick asked.

"Time will be the only answer to that question," Proster answered, "Until that point you will have to accept this is what has to be."

"I will be paying close attention to how your kingdom is doing while you deal with whatever it is," Garrick said, "Because we cannot afford for anything to happen that will result in harm."

"If you feel you must," Proster said, "But if you get in the way, I will confine you to your holding."

"Very well," Garrick said, but his voice and expression suggested otherwise.

"Dismissed," Proster's voice said the conversation was over. Garrick and Herwin left the throne room. Proster slumped down in his throne and put his head in his hands. Hertha could hear him sigh. He sat there for several more minutes. Finally he slowly got to his feet and went to his study door.

Hertha sat there for another minute before getting up and headed down the hallway. The lord from Grankle would be staying for a little while, which means his good looking servant would be around as well. Though a guard would be keeping an eye on him and it might make it difficult to get close to him, but if he was truly interested they would find a way.

Hertha headed for the dining room because it was

getting close to supper time. There was a crowd gathered already and waiting. Hertha sat at her usual table. Her father had always had the family sit in the dining room with the rest of the castle staff, but there was never any particular table for the family. Hertha's mother had always sat near her father, who sat at the raised table because everyone expected him to. Hertha and her siblings were never expected to sit with them. Zebulon usually sat at the table closest to the raised one with a book in one hand and utensil in the other. Narda had sat wherever there had been space by the time she arrived in the dining room because she was usually late. Hertha sat in the corner at the table where the kitchen staff sat. She would sit and listen to them. Occasionally Darwin would join her, but most of the time he was busy during official mealtimes and had to get leftovers from the head cook.

Tonight the table across from Zebulon's was full of people who were mostly unfamiliar to Hertha. She recognized the brown haired man, but the blond one, who she assumed was Lord Pardes, was not there. She wondered if he was too full of himself to eat with the rest of the people and stayed in his room when he found out he would not be dining at the king's table. The rest of the people at the table kept to themselves and they did not talk much to each other.

Ruana entered the dining room. She sat down at the table with Zebulon, which is what she usually did when Proster would not be eating. Most of the rest of the people there saw it in the same way Hertha did. Some of the new people looked at Ruana with some confusion. More of the staff members arrived and took their seats. Once everyone was settled the food was brought in. The kitchen staff delivered a plate to each person before sitting down with their own plates. Hertha was brought her plate when the staff sat down as usual. And everyone started to eat.

The conversation around the table was about an incident in the market place from three days ago. It had been the same conversation as the last couple days and the information was the same as before. Hertha knew a few more details, but they were not hers to share with anyone so she said nothing. Instead she spent the time looking around the room. Her mother and brother were in discussion, likely to be about the book sitting on the table beside Zebulon. Ruana probably never read the book, but she was good at picking apart arguments with logic and reason. She was one of the few people who could talk to Zebulon about all the knowledge he gained during his long days in the library. Hertha had never had the concentration to sit and read for that long, though she had read quite a few books from the castle library. She also found her brother spent way too much time in his head and not enough living in the real world; though his behaviour had changed in the last year. Hertha knew he was disappearing up to the tower for several hours a day instead of going to the library and he went without a book. However, she doubted he would venture any farther into the real world.

Hertha's eyes continued on and found herself looking into the brown eyes of the man at the table of the new people. He gave her a crooked half smile. She nodded back. The person next to him said something and he had to turn to them. He had to bow his head a little to hear the person. This time Hertha studied the rest of the people at the table. All, except one, were male, and the female was at the other end of the table from the brown haired man. The brown haired man wore the finer clothing of them all and was likely the assistant to Lord Pardes. Assistants were likely to be seen with the lord and thus would need clothing closer to the standard of the lord's clothing. That and if the brown haired man was headed for the kitchen earlier it was likely to ask that food be taken to Lord Pardes' room.

The person next to the brown haired apparently had a lot to say as the man did not look up again until Hertha had just about finished her supper. At which point the person on the other side of the man required his attention. With the noise level in the dining room, Hertha could understand the man having to get closer to the person talking. She did not know what Lord Pardes had set up at his holding, but only experience helped Hertha to hear the conversation around the table and tune the rest of the room out.

Hertha turned her attention to the rest of her supper. There was nothing else really interesting happening in the dining room for her to watch, so she might as well just eat. The kitchen staff had to eat slightly faster than the rest of the room and so they were finished about three bites ahead of Hertha. As soon as they were finished most of them were up and removing dishes from the table. They would go around the dining room and remove the dishes from the rest of the tables as people finished. Those who wanted to, or had time, could stay and talk as long as they wanted, but the kitchen staff could get to washing dishes a lot faster than if they waited until everyone cleared their own dishes. The kitchen staff had started doing this on their own after finding certain members of the castle staff would sit there and talk for up to three hours after the meal, which pushed the washing of dishes back by three hours or leave some poor soul at the dish pit until the last dish was delivered. Proster had not said a word of discouragement, so the process was continued to great success for the kitchen staff.

As soon as the kitchen staff were moving, it was also easier for Hertha to slip out and go wherever she wanted before anyone else was ready to leave. Today, she finished, but did not move right away. She waited until the brown haired man's eyes were on her before she got up and left the dining room. His eyes remained on her all the way to the door and as she turned left into the hallway.

Hertha headed down to the hallway to kitchen. There were only two people in the kitchen. The head cook and his son were sitting at the table near the ovens and did not even look up as Hertha went through it. She went through the kitchen door and out into the court yard. The only people in the courtyard were the usual guards who would eat later. Anyone who did not live at the castle had gone home, or wherever people went after work, so it was quiet.

Hertha sat down outside the kitchen door where she could see most of what was going on in the court yard. Not much happened until guards came out to relieve the ones there. A few people went across the court yard, but no one paid any attention to Hertha. No one was likely to be anywhere near the kitchen until the garbage would be taken out much later in the evening.

It was about half an hour before the brown haired man stepped out of the kitchen door. It closed behind him. The sun was getting low, but Hertha could still see him clearly. He looked down at her with those brown eyes filled with the same attraction filling her.

"Keften," the man offered his hand to Hertha.

"Hertha," Hertha took his hand. He helped her to her feet. They were just about touching. Neither let go of hands as they stood there, feeling drawn to each other, but both felt too exposed with the court yard. Hertha pulled him gently by the hand into an nearby alcove. The alcove was big enough for two people, out of sight of the court yard, and Hertha never figured out why it was built. But she was not thinking about any of that at the moment as Keften's lips touched hers.

Hertha snuck through the castle in her market place outfit. It had been a quiet week at the castle. When she sat up at her listening post, Hertha found her father was in no hurry to hear Lord Pardes' proposal. In fact, Proster was not seeing many people and only when scheduled at least a week before hand. So, Lord Pardes had a time scheduled, but it was going to be a two weeks away, which meant Keften was around and had free time to spend with Hertha. They had found places they could meet during the day when they would not be disturbed. It had been a good week as far as Hertha was concerned.

As she moved, she had to consciously keep the skip out of her step because it would get her noticed and Darwin would have given her a suspicious look when she got to him. She had been most of the week keeping the smile off her face, even though she was sure everyone could tell with the look in her eyes and the glow coming off her. However, the only times she was really around other people was at meal times and none of the kitchen staff were likely to mention anything to anyone. This would be the first time going to the market place since the day Lord Pardes and Keften arrived. When she had contacted Darwin, this was the first time all week he had time he could slip away for a few hours. Usually he was able to get away more than that, but apparently he had been really busy this week.

Hertha managed to get out the kitchen door without drawing attention and the court yard was easy to cross. She found Darwin leaning against the wall outside the gate as usual. He looked the same as always.

"Ready to go wandering?" Darwin asked when he saw her.

"Yes," Hertha answered putting her hand through his arm. They headed into the market place.

"I am surprised," Darwin said, "Your father has not kicked the nobleman out of the kingdom."

"He does not know why he has not done so himself," Hertha replied, "He does not plan to enter into any agreements with Grankle, but he had agreed to meet with Lord Pardes in two weeks. I do not know why and it sounds like he is not sure either."

"Completely strange," Darwin said, "Usually he is far more sure of himself."

"Right now he is having some trouble dealing with my sister's disappearance," Hertha said, "It is making him less sure of himself. He believes that if he had moved faster he could have stopped her from going after the demon. If he and his men had left half an hour earlier they would have been on the road before her. Now she has disappeared and he does not think she will be seen ever again."

"I can see how that would shake his confidence," Darwin said, "But what if Lord Pardes can convince him a trade agreement would benefit this kingdom?"

"Cannot happen," Hertha said, "My father has agreed to have Garrick in the room during the meeting to prevent any such things from happening."

"With Garrick in there, I would be amazed if Lord Pardes does not leave with the lecture on why there will never be a trade agreement ringing in his ears," Darwin said, "I am not sure why your father keeps him around as an adviser, but I would have gotten rid of him a long time ago."

"Garrick has been his advisor for a very long time," Hertha said, "My father has found ways of dealing with him and keeping him in line."

"That is a good thing for him," Darwin said, "He still makes a few others nervous."

"If he does anything, all you have to do is take it to my father," Hertha said, "Garrick will be straightened out in no time."

"It is still more relaxing when Garrick is out at his holding," Darwin said.

"Sometimes I think everyone finds it more relaxing when Garrick is out at his holding," Hertha replied.

"I smell some very delicious meat cooking," Darwin said turning down a street to their right, leading Hertha in the direction the smell was coming rom.

"You do not know if it is delicious, or not," Hertha said.

"No, but we should be able to find out shortly," Darwin gave Hertha a grin as he pulled her along. Hertha shook her head even as she smiled.

They found the meat seller half way down this street

and more than willing to sell them two slabs of meat cut off the large animal being rotated over a fire. They found a nearby cider seller before sitting down to enjoy it all. The meat tasted as good as it smelled and the cider was the perfect thing to follow it.

When they were done, Hertha and Darwin continued to wander the market place to see what else there was to see. They found a seller with some fruit pastries to finish off their meal. Other than that they did not see much they were interested in, so they headed back to the castle.

"That was a successful visit to the market," Darwin said.

"Very much indeed," Hertha said, "That was one of the best done meats I have ever tasted."

"It would be great if the cooks at the castle did meat like that," Darwin said.

"Everyone would eating a lot more and then have weight issues," Hertha said.

"But for the first while it would be worth it," Darwin said. Hertha laughed.

Suddenly Darwin pulled Hertha into alley way and they both pressed their backs to the wall.

"What is it?" Hertha kept her voice quiet.

"Two guards for Lord Pardes' party," Darwin answered, "I have seen them snooping around the castle."

"They should have some of our guards following them around," Hertha said.

"I think they lose their guard," Darwin said, pointing out of the alley way. Hertha looked around him and out into the street. The two men Darwin was pointing out were vaguely familiar as she had seen them at the dining table taken by the party for Grankle, but she had not paid any attention to them. However, the armour they were wearing had obviously been borrowed from the castle's armoury.

"Think they have permission to be wearing it?" Darwin asked once he saw Hertha's reaction of seeing the men.

"Loic would never have allowed it," Hertha answered, "Even if my father gave his permission. What have they been looking into at the castle?"

"No specific area," Darwin said, "Most of it has been general snooping."

"Have you been following them?" Hertha asked.

"Me and a few other members of the staff," Darwin answered, "We just have been sharing information about what has been going on."

"Told Loic, or anyone else?" Hertha asked.

"Not yet," Darwin answered, "Because when someone tried to tell Loic, there was no evidence they were up to no good, and we still have not found any. When we find some evidence, we will take all our knowledge to Loic."

"The men are just about out of sight," Hertha said, "If we are going to follow them, we have to do it now."

Darwin glanced at Hertha to see if she was serious. When he saw she was, Darwin grinned and glanced both directions before leading the way out of the alley.

PROSTER LEARNS HE HAS A SERIOUS PROBLEM

Proster listened to the two men explain their situation and what they wanted him to decide. As he listened, Proster's frustration grew. The whole situation could have been solved easily in the lower court, but Garrick or Herwin did not bother to deal with it. However, if he did not deal with it and properly, Garrick would be back with his 'serious' issue about the way Proster was ruling the kingdom. Proster was ready to suggest Garrick could enjoy the rest of Proster's rein from his holding.

The men fell silent and looked at Proster expecting a judgement. Proster had the judgement already set within a few minutes of listening to the men, so he recited it as if he just suddenly came to his conclusions when they had finished talking. The men were satisfied with his answer. They bowed and shuffled out. The guard watched Proster as they went passed him. Proster signalled for the guard to leave and close the door. The guard followed the order.

Proster sighed. He was too tired to deal with Garrick, but was going to have to. He felt too tired to get up and go to his office. But things still had to be done. Proster braced his arms on the arm rests and leveraged himself to his feet. Tiredness descended upon him like a bucket of water and he fell his knees. Proster held on to the arm rest until the dizziness went away. He needed to find somewhere to lie down for a few minutes.

Proster started forward again. The first few steps were not too bad, but the step off the dais was too much and his right knee gave out. Proster tried to catch himself, but blacked out before he hit the floor.

The smell of herbs came to Proster as he slowly regained consciousness. He was lying with his head raised on something fairly soft. He was trying to figure out what happened because he could not remember going to bed, or why his head would be raised.

"He is waking up," a deep voice above Proster said.

"Thank Saint Durward," the voice of the guard from the door came from nearby.

Proster slowly opened his very heavy eye lids. It felt like they were sealed closed, but he did manage it. He was lying on the couch in his study with a man he did not recognize standing over him and the guard standing by the door. The man had darker skin, grey eyes, dark hair, and clothing of good quality cloth that was worn in places without looking ratty. He was probably closed to six feet and average weight.

"Can you talk?" the stranger asked. Proster tried to ask what was going on, but his mouth felt too dry for any sound.

"Is there something to drink around here?" the stranger asked the guard.

"I do not know," the guard answered. Proster lifted his arm, which felt like there was a kite shield attached to it. He pointed toward the desk.

"In the desk?" the stranger asked. Proster nodded as best he could. The stranger went to the desk and started opening drawers. He came to the bottom drawer and took a bottle and glass out of it. After putting them on top of the desk, he opened the bottle and poured a small amount into the glass, which he brought over to Proster. Carefully, the stranger put the glass to Proster's lips and helped him take a drink. A little bit got down Proster's throat before the glass was taken away.

As he coughed, Proster could see the guard had his head bowed and his lips moving in a silent prayer. Proster gave in and closed his eyes as he continued to cough. Finally the coughing stopped and Proster focused his eyes opened again.

"Wha...happ..ed?" Proster could barely hear his own voice.

"Your heart gave out on you," the stranger said, "But your will to live is very strong. It is going to take a while before you have recovered enough to move."

"Do..n't...ell," Proster whispered.

"This kind of condition is very difficult to hide," the stranger said.

"But we will not say anything without your

permission," the guard added. The stranger glanced at the guard with some concern, but received a warning look in response.

"Very well," the stranger said, "But your condition is bad and there is very little I can do about it. For the most part rest and reduce the amount of pressure you are under."

Proster was not sure how he was supposed to do that, but he could no longer keep his eyes open. They closed and he drifted off again.

The strong smell of herbs pervaded the room as Proster became aware of his surroundings. He was lying on the couch in his office with the stranger sitting nearby. There was no one else in the room; even though Proster was pretty sure there had been someone else there earlier. The stranger looked up from the book he was reading.

"Can you talk?" the stranger asked. Proster thought about it for several minutes.

"What happened?" Proster asked.

"Your heart is failing you," the stranger answered, "But you have a very strong will to live."

"Who are you?" Proster asked.

"I am Dr. Kayson," the stranger answered, "Your guard called me here after he found you collapsed in the throne room. I am surprised he did not alert any other people in the castle."

"I appreciate his silence in the matter," Proster said as he slowly sat up. His head spun a little, but it was not too bad. There was a tingling in his left arm and the arm did not move properly, but Proster ignored it for now. His chest hurt a little and his throat was sore.

"Your condition is going to become self-evident fairly quickly to anyone paying attention," Dr. Kayson said, "You need a lot more rest and you cannot take on so much work if you are going to recover."

"If I do not follow your advice, how long do I have to live?" Proster asked as he stretched out his stiffened up right hand.

"A month at most," Dr. Kayson answered.

"Is there anything medicine that can help?" Proster asked.

"There are some herbs which have shown to give small improvements in people, but nothing has shown to extend life," Dr. Kayson answered.

"Is there anything else that can help?" Proster asked.

"I have never found anything," Dr. Kayson answered.

"Any other doctor around who would know something that would help?" Proster asked.

"Why not just rest and let your body heal?" Dr. Kayson asked, "You will live longer and likely better."

"I cannot afford to rest," Proster answered, "And I cannot afford to appear weak in any way. Even if it shortens my life, I need to carry on as if this never happened."

"I cannot help you kill yourself," Dr. Kayson said, "And the herbs I can offer you will not do enough good for what you need. However, I have a colleague who works with other things than just herbs. I do not think his methods will work to lengthen your live, but you can talk to him."

"Good," Proster said, "I will go change and then you can take me to him."

"You will have to move slow," Dr. Kayson said,

"And since you have not gotten enough rest there is a chance you will lose consciousness again."

"The clothing I want is tucked into a cabinet behind the desk," Proster said, "You can sit here and make sure I do not collapse."

"Very well," Dr. Kayson said.

Proster slowly got to his feet. He was a little light headed, but it was not too bad. However, he did not try to do anything at normal speed. He walked across the room and opened the cabinet. The clothing was tucked into the bottom shelf. Proster lowered himself into a squat. He gathered the cloth under his arm and used the shelves to pull himself out of the squat. Proster placed the clothing on the desk before closing the cabinet.

He stripped down to his underwear and placed his clothes on the desk chair. Putting on the clothes on was tiring and Proster found himself resting against the desk after pulling on the pants before even getting to the shirt. But he rested until he was no longer breathing hard and then continued. It took three times as longer than normal, but Proster was finally dressed in clothes he could go around the market place wearing without standing out.

Dr. Kayson sat in the chair and continued to read the book in his hand with an occasional glance up at Proster to make sure everything was all right. When Proster was resting he looked at the book, but did not recognize it so he figured Dr. Kayson brought it with him.

"I am ready," Proster said as he picked up one of the walking sticks from beside the door. Dr. Kayson closed the book, tucked it into the bag he had, and then stood up. Proster let him go through the door first. Dr. Kayson held the door until Proster was in the hallway before closing the door and starting down the hallway.

"Will the guards let us out?" Dr. Kayson asked, "Thane brought me in through the kitchen and through some secondary hallways."

"The guards have never stopped me from going in or out," Proster said, "Whether I am with someone else or not. They do not care if I go to the market place, or why I would have an interest in going to the market place, as long as I come back."

"They do not demand you take a guard with you?" Dr. Kayson asked.

"Most of them were once men under me," Proster answered, "They have seen me fight and feel no need to protect me in a place where having a guard would just bring me more attention of the wrong kind than do me any good."

"Very well," Dr. Kayson said.

They continued down the hallway to the main door. The guards on either side of the door watched them go, but did nothing to stop them. They walked across the court yard to the main gate without getting much more attention. Proster walked at a much slower pace than normal, but tried to make it appear he was merely matching his companion's pace. Dr. Kayson stayed at Proster's pace so they were matched. No one gave it even a second glance. They were able to go out the main gate without difficulty.

Once out on the streets, Dr. Kayson took the lead. They headed to the left of the gate, but did not go far enough to reach the gate on that side before going down one of the streets. The first two streets after the castle gate were those owned by lords and upper class, so the houses were large and there were plenty of servants around who were busy running errands. Proster and Dr. Kayson walked passed all of these houses to the next set of streets, which were houses owned by merchants and other middle class people. Dr. Kayson did not stop, pause, or even turn down any of these streets.

The next set of streets were shops and the market place. It was the middle street of this set that Dr. Kayson finally turned down. The walk was tiring to Proster, but they were going slow enough he was not likely to collapse. They went along this street until the city wall was visible at the far end. Most of these shops were the strange and weird destination shops that had few costumers due to lack of general knowledge of their existence. Dr. Kayson stopped in front of a two storey shop. Proster studied the shop for several minutes.

It was made out of the same stones as the rest of the houses on the street. However, someone had slathered the stones with reddish brown paint. The original coat had been uneven, there obviously had not been a second coat, and it had spent some years chipping off. There were two large glass windows on either side of the door which would have been used to display goods if they had not been painted over with black paint, which had not chipped and was evenly applied. The door was unpainted, but finished wood with a metal knocker and knob. The sign above the door may have been clear once, but the faded letters were just about gone with only a y and an n still visible. The upper storey had three smaller windows with black curtains preventing any view of the inside. There were no sounds coming from the shop and what little Proster could smell was mostly from the street, not the shop.

"Is he a doctor?" Proster asked.

"Yes," Dr. Kayson answered, "But he has wandered away from traditional medicine to other ways he claims heal. I would not usually bring anyone, or suggest anyone go to him, but it is likely the only place you will find answers."

"Then let us talk to him," Proster said waving toward the door. Dr. Kayson used the knocker and they waited. A few minutes went by before they heard a faint call sound like come in. Dr. Kayson opened the door and held it open for Proster. Proster entered the shop. It was dark in there and Proster stepped to one side to wait for his eyes to adjust. Dr. Kayson followed Proster inside and closed the door. Inside the shop there were several smells Proster did not recognize, but there did not appear to be any shelving or other such things. Instead there were chairs forming a circle in the middle of the room and a doorway with a curtain over it about the middle of the shop. On the floor the lines from where the counter had been were still visible. No one was currently in the room and the only sound was water dripping somewhere at the back of the shop.

Proster glanced at Dr Kayson, but received a wait for it look in return. Unsure exactly what to do, Proster turned back around. There was still no one in view. Proster took a few steps farther into the shop and still looking around. With his eyes having adjusted, he noticed all of the chairs had a symbol painted on the back. He could only see some of the symbols, but they all looked like ones he had seen in a book on magic for amateurs. The author of the book had been an amateur in his knowledge of magic as far as Proster had been able to tell after reading it and Proster had never been much of an expert in the area.

"Good afternoon," the voice had a slight feminine quality to it. Proster looked up at the man who had stepped out from behind the curtain. The man was so thin he appeared to be skin stretched over bone and organs. Proster was almost sure he could see the man's teeth under the skin around his lips. The man wore a ruby robe with more symbols stitched into it with gold thread, which was too big for him. He had a shock of brown hair standing straight up and wide blue eyes.

"Good afternoon, Beynon," Dr. Kayson said.

"What can I help you with?" Beynon asked folding his hands and resting them at his waist.

"My heart is failing, according to Dr. Kayson," Proster answered, "But I cannot afford to take the time to rest in the manner he suggests and I am looking for alternative ways to treat my condition."

"You came to the right place," Beynon said. He smiled without showing his teeth and it looked awkward. "Have a seat and we can discuss it."

"At the moment I prefer to stand," Proster said.

"The symbols will do nothing to harm you," Beynon said, "They lack any power to affect you in anyway."

"I have learned to be careful around such things," Proster said, "So you will have to excuse my hesitation."

"Understandable," Beynon said, "Many people who come in here have similar notions. I suppose we can stand if we must." Beynon waved toward a small amount of empty space to his right. Proster and Dr. Kayson moved when he did so they stood facing each other.

"How long have you had symptoms of this heart

condition?" Beynon asked.

"A couple weeks I believe," Proster answered.

"But no serious symptoms until today?" Beynon asked.

"No," Proster answered.

"Hold out your wrist, please," Beynon said. Proster did. Beynon put two fingers on the pulse point and rested them there. Proster expected Beynon's fingers to be icy cold, but instead they were warm. Beynon appeared to be listening. After about three minutes he removed his fingers and Proster dropped his arm back to his side.

"You are very lucky to be alive," Beynon said, "Most of the time such serious symptoms end up causing the person to die. However, it also means Dr. Kayson is right about you resting or your life will be significantly shortened."

"Is there anything you can do about it?" Proster asked.

"There are two methods I can offer to you," Beynon answered, "Neither are guaranteed, but I believe they should work for you."

"What are they?" Proster asked.

"I will be right back," Beynon replied, "Wait here." Beynon turned and went back through the doorway. He ducked under the curtain and it was possible to see what was back there.

"You do not believe his methods can work," Proster kept his voice low.

"I believe in medicine," Dr. Kayson replied, "And what Beynon is going to offer you is not medicine as I have ever known it. If either solution works it is more likely to be luck than anything else."

"I have seen magic work where medicine never could," Proster said.

"I have never seen magic work at all," Dr. Kayson said, "And I hardly believe that it can replace medicine."

"Which is why we are here," Proster said.

"Just be wary of whatever methods Beynon comes up with," Dr. Kayson said, "His belief in alternate ways of healing can have some very questionable outcomes and making you sicker is a possibility."

Proster did not have time to respond before the curtain moved and Beynon came back. In his left hand he held a glass bottle full of a white powder and in his right hand was a black cord with a pendant on it. He came over to Proster and Dr. Kayson. First he held up the cord.

"This is a bloodstone pendant," Beynon said. The pendant was tear drop shaped dark green rock with red lines and dots through it.

"It helps the blood circulation in your body," Beynon said, "Which should help your heart. All you have to do it wear it around your neck and keep it close to your heart."

Proster took the pendant, but did not say anything. Dr. Kayson did not say anything, but it was obvious he did not believe a pendant could do anything to help with Proster's heart.

"This is a powder made from-," Beynon said.

"I do not think it would be helpful knowing what exactly the powder is made from," Dr. Kayson interrupted Beynon. Beynon stopped his explanation and thought about it for a minute.

"Very well," Beynon said, "You add two spoon fills

to a glass of water and drink two glasses a day, one in the morning and one just before bed. Do not take any more than that, or it may decrease your heart rate causing you other problems. Too little will not have the same amount of effect, which can result in your current symptoms not going away." Beynon handed the bottle to Proster, who looked it over. The powder was too small to tell what exactly it had been before it was ground up.

"If you need more of either you can come back," Beynon said as he wiped his hands on his robe.

"How much do I owe you for this?" Proster asked.

"Nothing," Beynon answered, "I do not make money off my cures."

"Then thank you for this," Proster said.

"I hope they help you," Beynon said.

Dr. Kayson led the way out of the shop. Out on the street, Proster tucked the glass bottle and the pendant away in the cloak before they started back along the street.

"I doubt the pendant will have too much effect," Dr. Kayson said, "But I would advise you to be very careful with the powder."

"Sometimes the best thing is to know all the information to make such decisions easier," Proster said.

"Would you want to know if the powder is made from some animal's intestines?" Dr. Kayson asked, "Because that is the kind of powders Beynon usually deals in. I think it is easier to take such things if the origins are not known."

"And yet you do not believe it will work as it is supposed to," Proster said, "Even believing it will make things worse." Dr. Kayson shrugged in response rather than say anything.

They continued up the street. It was not long before they reached the street where they turned the corner and headed back up toward the castle. It was the same distance they had walked before and they were walking at the same pace as they had on the way down, but somehow it seemed to take less time to walk back to the castle. Dr. Kayson hesitated ever so slightly walking back through the main gate into the court yard and the main door to the castle as if worried the guards would tell him he was not allowed in. The guards remained at their posts and merely watched as Proster and Dr. Kayson entered the castle.

Proster led the way back to his study. On arriving Proster sat down in the desk chair and put the items Beynon had given him on the desk.

"You will not tell anyone about my condition," Proster said.

"As you requested," Dr. Kayson said.

"If anyone finds out, I know it was you who told people," Proster said, "Because Thane will never tell a living soul, even under threat of torture. But I also need you to tell me if I am getting closer to the end of my life, or whether there is still some distance."

"I can check on you once a day," Dr. Kayson said.

"Come during the evenings," Proster said, "The guards will let you in."

"Then I will see you tomorrow evening," Dr. Kayson said, "As I do not believe there is anything else I can do for you today."

"Very well," Proster said, "See you tomorrow."

Dr. Kayson left the study and closed the door behind

him. Proster watched until the door closed. Then he rested his elbows on the desk and put his head in his hands.

Proster was not sure how long he had sat there when there was a knock on the door.

"Come in," Proster called. The door opened and Garrick entered the study. He closed the door behind him.

"You had an appointment scheduled for this afternoon," Garrick said, "Everyone was there, except you. Apparently you went to the market place with an unknown person."

"I do not remember any scheduled appointments for this afternoon," Proster said, "When was it set up?"

"Yesterday when the rest of the appointments were set up," Garrick said.

"The page from yesterday had no appointments for this afternoon," Proster said, "If there had been something written in, I would have been there. However, you have been leaving cases the lower courts can take care of and expecting me to be places with limited notice lately which makes me suspect this afternoon's appointment was not actually scheduled."

"It was scheduled," Garrick said, "Herwin and I had to figure out how to explain to them why the king was not available to see them."

"Because he was busy dealing with something else," Proster said, "And had no notice of the appointment. I am going to give you an option. You can stay in the city and only do work in the lower court without any other activities under your control. Or you can go to your holding until told otherwise."

"I just told you the appointment was scheduled," Garrick said.

"And I just gave you an option of which you want to do," Proster said, "Pick one, or I will pick it for you."

"I am not-" Garrick started.

"I do not care!" Proster stood up and banged his fist on the desk. Garrick backed up a step and fear came into his eyes.

"I am the King of Proster!" Proster said, "And you will obey me!"

Garrick did not say anything, or move. Proster felt his body was shaking and his heart rate was going up. He was getting light headed and could feel nauseous. Black spots drifted into his vision.

Proster dropped his hands to his side and took a deep breath. He tried to get his heart rate down a little bit. Garrick did not attempt to do anything to fill the time or space as they stood opposite each other.

"Get out of here," Proster ordered. Garrick was out of the study in under a minute with the door closed behind him. Proster collapsed into the chair. He spent his energy trying to get his heart rate down so the rest of the symptoms would go down.

Proster almost lost consciousness several times as he sat there and concentrated on surviving the moment. It was slow, but he did eventually get his heart rate under control. The symptoms went away enough for Proster to get up and made his way slowly to the couch. He settled down on the couch. He needed to figure out what to do.

He could not abdicate to his son at the moment. He could not tell anyone about his problem because of Lord Pardes' presence. If Grankle learned about his condition they would try to use it to come in and take over. Garrick and Herwin were going to send him to his grave faster with their attempts to get his mind back on ruling the kingdom. The kingdom needed a king. His family needed him. He was not ready to die just yet. But he was not sure about using the pendant, or mystery powder. But everyone seemed to have decided he could not rest and recover.

Proster closed his eyes and sighed. He was not sure he was going to survive much longer.

FOLLOWING THE GUARDS AROUND THE CITY AND PROSTER'S MEETING WITH LORD PARDES

Hertha and Darwin were careful to keep the men in sight without following them close enough to be spotted. The guards followed the wall of the city and checked it at the end of every street. They spent some time studying the main gate to the city out of sight of the city guards standing there. Then they moved on to the city wall on the other side.

"Are they looking for a weakness in the wall or something?" Darwin asked.

"It looks like it," Hertha answered, "But they are not likely to find any. Even my father did not get through the wall anywhere except the front gate and there the men had help from rebels in the city."

"So, it was fairly easy for him," Darwin said.

"No," Hertha said, "His men came in through the

front gate. He and two of his men snuck in to secure the castle and make the whole invasion easier."

"How did he get in?" Darwin asked.

"Not in any way they are going to find," Hertha answered with a smirk.

They continued to follow Lord Pardes' guards as the guards followed the wall back up to the wall around the court yard.

"This city is made for defending," Hertha said as they watched the two guards disappear into the armoury, "I very much doubt they can find any weaknesses."

"But the fact they are doing things in disguise means they are up to something," Darwin said, "They may have lots of other plans."

"Let me know how things are going," Hertha said.

"I will," Darwin said, "Hopefully there will be enough evidence to take to Loic before they do anything serious."

"I really hope so," Hertha said, "Shall we go back out to the market place in a few days?"

"I think I have some time in a couple days," Darwin said.

"I will wait to hear from you then," Hertha said.

"Okay," Darwin said.

Hertha headed for the kitchen door while Darwin headed toward the stables. No one in the kitchen paid attention to Hertha as she went through it to the hallway beyond. Today she did not run into Keften, but it was still closer to the middle of the afternoon than evening and he did not usually come down to give the request for Lord Pardes to have his supper served in his room until later.

As she passed the throne room she saw Garrick and a man standing there as if waiting for her father. Her interest suddenly piqued, Hertha changed her destination. She headed up to her listening post. The men were still in the throne room when she got there and sat down near the edge. There were quiet as they stood and waited.

"His majesty knew about the appointment, right?" the man asked.

"We talked it over with him yesterday," Garrick said, "He should have it marked down."

"We have been here for half an hour," the man said, "Perhaps, his majesty has forgotten it."

"It appears so," Garrick said. He went toward the door to the hallway and pushed the door open the rest of the way open. The guard standing there turned to look at him because Garrick did not exit the room.

"Thane, where is King Proster?" Garrick asked.

"He has been called away to see to something else," Thane answered.

"He is not in the castle?" Garrick asked, "What was he called away to deal with?"

"I have not been informed as to what," Thane answered, "Merely that it was important."

"Do you know when he will return?" Garrick asked.

"I do not," Thane answered.

"It is fine," the man said, "I understand if our king had more important things he was needed for. My issue can wait until the next time his majesty has time to listen to me. Thank you for your time and let me know when I can come back."

"I am sorry about this," Garrick said. The man left the throne room. Garrick went to the door to Proster's study and tried to open it. It was locked. Thane stood there and watched Garrick. Hertha figured he must have known something, but he would never say anything to Garrick, or anyone else. Garrick did not even bother to ask Thane anymore questions as he stalked out of the throne room.

Hertha waited a few minutes before getting up and headed to her room. She changed back into her regular clothes before going to the dining room. Supper was fairly normal, but Proster never showed up and Ruana did not seem to know he would not be there. Only when she saw he was not sitting at the raised table did she sit down at the same table as Zebulon.

Hertha paid more attention to the table of people from Grankle tonight. Keften was not there, but he had told Hertha that Lord Pardes was going to require his attention all day. However, the guards were there. Hertha watched the interaction between the guards and the rest of the people. The guards sat on one end of the table and there was enough space between them and the rest for another person to sit there. The guards did not talk to anyone else or each other. They were too concentrated on the food to bother with anything else. They did not seem to be concerned about anyone else in the room. They did not even look up at the feeling of Hertha watching them.

The rest of the group had gotten used to being in Proster and were comfortable with each other. They talked to each other and ignored most of the rest of the room. Since everyone else had gotten used to strangers in the dining room and were ignoring the people from Grankle, it worked out. It was only the two guards who sat silently without interacting with anyone. No one else seemed to have noticed the guards' behaviour, until Hertha noticed one of the stable hands at a table near the door to the dining room. The stable hand kept glancing at the guards, but did not stare. If Hertha had not been paying attention, she would not have noticed the stable hand's interest in the guards. But the guards were not likely to do anything in the dining room, so Hertha went back to paying attention her own meal.

The next two weeks had little for excitement happening. Hertha saw Keften as much as they both could. She went to the market place with Darwin three times. Darwin had very little to report on the guards from Grankle as the guards had done nothing more than snoop around the castle and the city. Since Darwin had told the rest of the group about the guards changing outfit it was much harder for them to go around unsupervised.

Hertha spent time up at her listening post. Her father had continued to only see those who had appointments and even those appeared to be carefully chosen. The man with the missed appointment did finally get his time in front of King Proster. Hertha did notice Garrick's absence at all of the proceedings, but she knew he was still in the castle because she saw him occasionally in the hallways and dealing with things involving the lower court. Even without Garrick putting pressure on her father, he still appeared tired and moved a lot slower than normal. But that was only during court hours. Hertha did not see Proster at any other time, which was strange because he usually made sure he spent some time with his children during a week. Hertha had missed the hours she and her father usually spent talking, especially since he had not even sent a message as to why he was not there.

The day Lord Pardes was supposed to meet with King Proster, Hertha made sure she was not needed for anything and settled herself at her listening post as early as possible. Proster usually got to the throne room early when there was an important meeting in the throne room, but today he was nowhere in sight when Garrick and Herwin arrived in the throne room. They took their places on either side of the throne and waited. Extra guards arrived and took place on the inside of the door to the throne room. That was everyone who was from Proster who would be in the throne room during the meeting. It was unknown how many people from the Grankle group would be in the throne room for the meeting. Hertha knew Keften would be there because he had told Hertha that he would not be available during this time.

Proster opened the door from his study mere minutes before the meeting was supposed to start. He moved slowly to the throne using one of the decorative walking sticks to help him. Both Garrick and Herwin looked concerned, but Proster ignored them. Garrick had tensed as Proster had gotten closer to the dais, but relaxed a little when Proster did not even glance his direction. Proster sat down like an old man with multiple issues. Hertha watched as he used his right hand to adjust his left on the arm of the chair. Neither Garrick nor Herwin seemed to notice it, but Hertha felt as if she was in danger of watching her father die during this meeting.

Herwin stepped forward and said something quietly into Proster's ear. Proster just waved him away. Herwin stepped back and exchanged glances with Garrick, but neither of them said anything else.

The doors to the throne room opened and Lord Pardes entered with Keften a step behind and to the left of him. Keften had a rolled up scroll and a board with a fresh piece of paper on it. They came down the carpet to the appropriate place and bowed. The guards closed the doors behind them.

"Lord Pardes of Grankle and assistant," the guard from the inside of the door announced while Lord Pardes and Keften were bowing.

"You may rise," Proster said. His voice was the same strong tone Hertha was used to, which relieved her somewhat. She noticed Garrick also relaxed a little bit.

"Thank you, your majesty, for granting us an audience," Lord Pardes said once he had straightened. His hair was perfectly done and the blue material his outfit was made from looked like it was velvet. His neck and shoulders kept his head straight and gave him the appearance of someone trying to be taller than he actually was. There was confidence coming off him in waves and if he had been in a room with anyone else his presence might have been slightly overwhelming. However, even somewhat sickly, Proster's presence was overpowering and it was higher since he wanted Lord Pardes to feel smaller.

"My time is limited," Proster said, "And you said you would take up as little of it as possible."

"That is correct," Lord Pardes replied, "The people the King of Grankle have sent before me have brought extravagant trading agreements for your consideration and refusal. There is nothing Grankle has the people in

Proster need and nothing for which any trading agreement hold any appeal. I am here, not to tempt you with something you do not need, but to discuss the possibility of removing the ban current in place on all trade between the kingdoms."

"The ban was put into place as a safety measure," Proster said, "Because Grankle kept sending things which were intended to harm the residents of Proster and I have to do what I can to protect my people."

"Your logic and reasoning for the ban is completely understood," Lord Pardes said, "I am here to see if we can set boundaries within which trade can proceed with limited to no harm falling on either side."

"And you have some suggestion to start with," Proster said.

"Indeed," Lord Pardes said as he held out his hand to Keften without looking back. Keften placed the scroll into Lord Pardes' hand, "These have been agreed on by the King of Grankle and hopefully a starting point for discussion." Lord Pardes held the scroll up, but did not move forward. Herwin stepped to Lord Pardes and took he scroll, which he delivered to Proster before taking his position again. Proster broke the seal on the scroll before unrolling it. Lord Pardes waited patiently as Proster read through what was on the scroll. Herwin and Garrick stood in their position with minimal twitching. Keften, however, had difficulty staying still and was practically dancing in place in comparison. Hertha figured he had spent a limited amount of time in a throne room, let alone one where he was not exactly welcomed.

Finally Proster rolled the scroll up and looked up at Lord Pardes.

"Some very interesting starts for discussion," Proster said, "But nothing guarantees the safety of my people if these guidelines are followed. There are several blatant loop holes in here that means Grankle will be safe while Proster is in harm's way."

"This start is merely what was brought up during the discussion in Grankle," Lord Pardes said, "It is this discussion with which safety of Proster in the prime concern."

"I think you have jumped several steps ahead of where the current discussion is," Proster said, "There is no motivation for Proster to create such an agreement with Grankle, especially since the trading ban was put into place by Proster to protect the citizens of Proster."

"There are several merchants who have asked for this agreement," Lord Pardes said, "And not all of them are on the Grankle side of the shared border. I know your time is limited and you can easily just send me home, but there have been requests to have an agreement set up to let trade return between those merchants. I am here because of them, not because the King of Grankle has asked me to be. As such I am very much hoping you will at least entertain the idea of such an agreement and let the discussion happen. If we cannot come up with an agreement which suits both sides, I can take back word to those merchants that it was attempted, but will never be. They will perhaps then leave the issue alone and any other representative from Grankle on a trade mission can be sent back with a shoe print on their backside."

"I have not heard anything about merchants from Proster looking for business in Grankle," Proster said.

"I am prepared for such a case," Lord Pardes said as

he took a packet of letters out of his pocket and offered it to Proster. Herwin once again stepped down to get the letters and deliver them to Proster before taking up his position again. Proster slipped one of the letters out and opened it. He read through it while everyone else waited.

"Are they all similar to this?" Proster asked holding up the letter after he finished reading it.

"Indeed," Lord Pardes said.

"Then you have the floor to what you believe would be useful points of discussion for Proster, should Proster decide to foolishly enter into an agreement to lift certain parts of the trade ban," Proster replied.

The discussion from there took a more complicated turn and Hertha found herself bored from it all. She understood good portions of what they were talking about, but trade agreements were like talking to her brother about one of his books. She usually did not do it for fun or entertainment, but only if she was forced to due to being unable to get out of it. She did, however, continue to sit and listen. Her father, who had looked so ill at the beginning of the meeting, did not tire as easily as Hertha feared, but kept the discussion lively. The meeting did not change how he looked. Garrick and Herwin grew tired long before Proster did. Keften managed to not look tired through the whole thing, but Hertha was not entirely sure he was not playing games on the paper in between making notes on what was said.

When lunch time arrived, Proster and Lord Pardes agreed to meet again in the next open spot available in Proster's schedule. It was the first time in over hour Herwin and Garrick paid attention to what was going on. The next time available was in a week and Lord Pardes agreed to it. Hertha was okay with it because it meant Keften would not be going home very soon and would have plenty of time to spare. Lord Pardes and Keften left the throne room and the guards were immediately dismissed.

"You were talking about seriously making a trade agreement with Grankle," Herwin said.

"I was," Proster replied, "And if you two are getting into a snit about it, then Lord Pardes obviously believes it might happen as well."

"But?" Herwin said.

"The merchant who are writing letters have much better things to do with their time," Proster said, "They just do not want to change how they do business. They will get over it. And the longer Lord Pardes is here the more time I have to figure out why I let him stay in the first place."

"As long as there is no real agreement being made," Herwin said.

"You both can attend all the meetings," Proster said, "And you both can make sure I do not sign any trade agreement with Grankle."

"Very well," Herwin said. He and Garrick stepped down off the dais. They left the throne room. Proster stayed where he was even once the doors to the throne room were closed. Hertha waited as well. Finally Proster slowly got to his feet and headed for his study. Only once the door was closed and he was inside did Hertha get up. She headed for the dining room.

There were no plans in place for the afternoon and Keften was busy, so Hertha went to the library to find a book. Zebulon was not there because it was his usual hour to be in the high tower. No one else was there when Hertha entered. The large window gave the room enough light that even going into the far shelves did not require a lamp. Hertha went three shelves to the right of the door. She had a good idea what book she wanted because she had thought about reading it for a couple months.

Hertha had found the book and was just about to take it off the shelf when she heard the door to the library open. She froze and listened. Zebulon was not going to be back for another forty five minutes. Proster was locked in his study and would not come out until the next scheduled meeting. Ruana had gone into the city for her usual volunteer time. No one else in the castle was likely to come into the library.

Hertha felt fear travel up her spine. She did not know why. The door closed, but there was no sound from anyone else in the room. Hertha held her breath. There was no sound of a person in the room, but she could feel their presence. She inched as quietly as she could to the end of the shelf to peer around at the doorway. There was no one is sight.

The spot near the shelf that was left of the door and going toward the window squeaked with someone's weight. Hertha's breath caught in her throat. Whoever it was moved farther away from the shelf to avoid the next squeaky spot. That suggested to her she did not want to face the person, because there was no reason to sneak around the castle library. There was only one thing Hertha could think to do.

She moved quietly and with an eye out for the other person. She ducked between the shelves if she heard them moving close to where they could see her. And for the first time in her life, Hertha was glad for the squeaky wooden floor of the library. She reached the back wall of the library, which were cabinets instead of shelves. Hertha pulled open one of the bottom doors. All the cabinets were empty, and Hertha never figured out what they were built for anyway. Several of them were big enough for her to fit in, but several of them were locked and she did not have the key. Carefully and quietly Hertha folded herself into the cabinet and closed the door behind her. Once inside Hertha was able to lock the door. It would not lock her in, but the person outside would need a key. From inside the cabinet, the squeaks of the floor were slightly muffled, but she could still hear them.

The person went all the way to the other side of the library going around all the shelves. Then the person started back across and then around the shelves on this side of the room. The squeaks reached the cabinets and the person moved around. Hertha heard some of the cabinet doors open, but it was not even all the cabinets that were unlocked. Hertha wanted to see the person, but if she opened the door the person would have noticed and she could be in trouble.

The person seemed to give up and Hertha could hear a few squeaks heading back to the door. The person stepped on as many squeaky spots they had found. Hertha did not move and worked to keep her breathing as quiet as possible. There was no sound of the door opening and the person leaving. In fact the squeaky spots only went a couple shelves over from the cabinets and not as far as the door.

There were no sounds in the library for ten minutes. Hertha had spent hours in the library as a child and was used to playing hide and seek in these cabinets. She and her siblings would spend hours at a time in these cabinets. With that and picking one with more than enough space for herself, Hertha was actually quite comfortable. If the person was waiting for her to get scared or nervous enough to open the door, they could end up waiting a long time if hunger did not eventually bring her out. The person did not move for another ten minutes and Hertha was starting to feel tired. She kept having to remind herself there was someone out there, so she would not fall asleep.

Then Hertha heard the door to the library open. It must have been Zebulon coming back. There was no squeak, but the person must have moved out of sight because Zebulon did not greet anyone as he moved toward the window. His favourite chair was in front of the window with his back turned to the rest of the library. Concern for Zebulon flashed through Hertha's mind, but there was nothing she could do about it from her current position. She did not have any way to the door to get help and she had no weapon she could use on the person. Zebulon settled in his chair.

Time past, but Hertha could not hear anyone moving, though she could occasionally hear her brother making comments or laughing at what he was reading. Then there was a squeak just short of the door, which could not have been her brother. Zebulon did not appear to have heard it as he continued with his current commentary. The door opened as softly as possible and closed with the same amount of noise. Zebulon still did not notice, but Hertha knew he spent way too much time in his head and books to notice many things.

Hertha carefully pulled herself out of the cabinet and

looked around. There was no one in sight. She wondered who the person was, but it was too late to find out. Going back to the shelf, Hertha took the books she wanted. She went to the main sitting area which was in front of the window and separated the shelves on the left from the shelves on the right. Zebulon was sitting in his chair completely absorbed in his book. She sat down in a chair half way between Zebulon and the door. After glancing around for anyone else sneaking around the library and not seeing any, she opened the book and started reading.

PROSTER LEARNS A LOT ABOUT HIS CONDITION AND THAT HE NEEDS TO MAKE SOME DECISIONS

Proster sat in his desk chair and stared at the bottle of white powder sitting on top of the paper work. There was a knock on the door of his study.

"Who is it?" Proster called.

"Dr. Kayson," came the response.

"Come in," Proster called. The door opened and Dr. Kayson stepped into the room before closing the door behind him.

"How do you feel today?" Dr. Kayson asked as he took a seat in one of the chairs.

"Worse than I have before," Proster answered, "Though I do not think it has anything to do with my condition."

"Worse in what ways?" Dr. Kayson asked.

"I no longer wish to leave my office," Proster

answered, "I am seeing these walls as my protection. I think about things I enjoyed outside these walls, things like spending time with my family and going for walks in the sunshine, and I find I no longer am interested in doing them. Any energy I had left after the first attack is gone with nothing but the want to lie on the couch and forget the rest of the world. Worries I never bothered with fill my mind and eat away at it. I feel weighed down."

"You are describing a mental issue which is known to affect many people who have suffered such things as you have," Dr. Kayson said, "There are ways to deal with such symptoms but it will not be easy, especially with everything else you are dealing with. Did you take Beynon's powder?" Dr. Kayson seemed to notice the bottle of powder on the desk.

"For two days," Proster answered, "But I stopped and am not sure what to do with the rest of the powder."

"How well did the powder work?" Dr. Kayson asked.

"Not well," Proster answered, "It made my throat sore and I started seeing insects when there were no insects in the room. The second day I started feeling the insects were crawling all over me at which point I did not take any more."

"Were those the only hallucinations?" Dr. Kayson asked.

"The only one I experienced," Proster answered.

"Do you have any issues with insects?" Dr. Kayson asked.

"Never in my life," Proster answered.

"Did you try the pendant?" Dr. Kayson asked.

"Yes," Proster said showing Dr. Kayson the pendant cord, "There have been no symptoms connected to it."

"Has it helped with any symptoms from your condition?" Dr. Kayson asked.

"Not that I can tell," Proster answered, "Can you take the powder back to Beynon?"

"I can," Dr. Kayson said.

"Then you can tell me how to deal with the symptoms I am experiencing you claim is a mental issue," Proster said.

"You are depressed," Dr. Kayson said, "You have convinced yourself you cannot return to your normal behaviour due to your condition for fear it will make things worse. This anxiety is making you lose your interest in life and living, which I believe was what you wanted to do and the reason I am not to tell anyone what is going on. I am sure other people have noticed your condition by now and are worried or seeing your weakness. You have to live despite your condition if you wish to get rid of those symptoms."

"You told me to rest," Proster said.

"I told you to rest for a couple days," Dr. Kayson said, "I did not tell you to give up your life due to the condition. At this point you have wasted two weeks of your life, shortened your life with worrying about it all, and has not hidden it from anyone. You need to go back to living your life and deal with the condition. You survived because you had the strength to live. You need to use that strength or your condition will take you faster."

"I see," Proster said, "And how will I know if my condition is deteriorating?"

"Tiredness, dizziness, chest pain, weakness, changes

in pulse, collapsing suddenly, blacking out, and mental decline," Dr. Kayson answered.

"Mental decline as in forgetfulness?" Proster asked.

"Mental decline usually comes after a black out due to your body suffering from lack of air," Dr. Kayson answered, "The lack of air appears to be destroying parts of your mind and forgetting things can be part of that, but so can losing the ability to use parts of your body such as you have with your left hand. There is also losing skills you have had for years."

"So, I become a half working body with no inner workings left," Proster said.

"After enough black outs it is possible," Dr. Kayson said, "But it is far more likely one of the black outs will kill you before that happens. You could also recovery from some of the symptoms with proper treatment."

Proster sat without speaking for several minutes. Dr. Kayson left him to it and dug into his bag for the book he carried with him. He had gotten used to Proster spending time thinking without the need to speak and used the time the best way he knew how. There was no outward sign of the direction of Proster's thoughts, but occasionally he would run his right hand over his left.

He had never been truly sick in his life since he was very young. Fever had come through the kingdom and wiped out a good percentage of the population. A couple servants brought it into the castle without suffering from it themselves. Most of the royal family had been spared even then. Proster and his youngest brother had both gotten sick. Proster remembered lying helplessly in bed as his body burned. The only servant allowed in the room to keep the fever from spreading kept replacing the blanket when Proster kicked it off.

The blanket would be tucked back in and he would have to fight his way loose. The window had been closed to keep ill air out and prevent further suffering. When Proster was aware enough he would demand water, as much as he could drink. The servant usually hesitated every time he asked and would only give it in small quantities, but gave his brother only the amount the doctor had suggested. Proster had survived intact and had never been sick since then. His brother never truly recovered from the fever, though the symptoms went away. A servant always had to be present to make sure Proster's brother did not collapse or get hurt. It was only when the boy grew up and met the woman he would marry did his health improve. Proster had figured it to be partially because she thought fresh air and exercise good for him.

Now Proster sat in his desk chair and was sick for the second time in his life. The illness would eat at his body and his mind until it killed him outright. He had many things to live for and many things he still needed to do. Dr. Kayson had not given him a timeline as to when the symptoms would get worse, but Proster doubted it included the word years. There had been words of recovery, but how much and how long were unknown. He could continue to sit in his office, scared to step outside with the possibility someone might see him black out, and not finish what he needed to do before he died. Or he could go back to his normal duties, take Dr. Kayson advice on how to recover, and possibly have more time to get things done.

Proster had fought for his current life and succeeded. This weight that had moved into his life suggested the fight was over and it was time to give up. If the weight had been an enemy, Proster would have cut it in half without a second thought and moved on to more important enemies. And mentally that was what he was going to have to do.

"So, what are your suggestions for recovery?" Proster asked as he pulled the pendant off and tossed it to sit next to the bottle of white powder.

"Exercise is one of your best starting point," Dr. Kayson answered putting down the book, "Your left arm will not recover until you work with it to get it back to former strength, but it must be done slowly. You will have to take some time at the beginning and end of your day to relax. This requires you to leave all work here in you study and not take it to any rooms you use for relaxation. You need to get eight to nine hours of sleep at night without interruption. Exercise for the rest of your body is also important. I recommend walking to start, but it is up to you. Do not start with activity that is too strenuous because it will make you more likely to have another black out. Alcohol must be cut down to once a day and the rest of the time you should be drinking water. Pick vegetables over bread a mealtimes and avoid large amounts of fat with your meats."

"Is that it?" Proster asked when Dr. Kayson paused.

"It is a good start," Dr. Kayson answered, "Anything else would be better to wait until after we know how those changes affect your body. If the symptoms decrease then just continued doing what I suggested and if they do not decrease then we will have to see what else you need to change."

"It sounds like a lot," Proster said.

"Start into it all slowly," Dr. Kayson said, "Slow

gives your body time to adjust to the changes and should give you enough progress so you do not give up on the whole thing."

"Very well," Proster said, "You can take Beynon's stuff back to him and I will try it your way."

"Medicine has shown itself to be the best approach to many medical conditions," Dr. Kayson said, "Much better than magic."

"You live in a world where magic has been limited," Proster said, "If the magical energy was stronger than medicine might be second best."

"I am unlikely to live anywhere there is more magical energy," Dr. Kayson said, "So, I find medicine much more helpful."

"At this moment, the only thing that will work is medicine," Proster said, "As Beynon will figure out shortly. If the magical energy was the same as it was a couple months ago, then his cures might have worked. The magical energy in this area was high until then. So, you have lived in an area with high magical energy. However, there has not been anyone within the area who is strong enough in magical abilities to cure medical issues. If there had been someone in that position you may have a different position as well as have a lot less patients."

"What made the magical energy go away?" Dr. Kayson asked.

"Closing the magical portal by the current portal guardian," Proster answered.

"How do you know that?" Dr. Kayson asked.

"Because that is where Narda ended up," Proster answered, "She ended up on the other side of the portal and in the role of portal guardian. To avoid any more magical beings getting through she closed the portal in a way nothing can go through either way."

"That sounds like she cannot come back either," Dr. Kayson said.

"She has to stay where she is and be the portal guardian," Proster said.

"Your grieving is likely part of what caused your initial black out," Dr. Kayson said, "Losing a child is one of the hardest things that can happen to a parent. Your daughter may not have died, but you did lose her. How is your wife dealing with the loss?"

"When I last talked to her, she was sad, but accepting of the situation," Proster said, "But she has always taken things easier than anyone else I have ever met."

"Did she grieve?" Dr. Kayson asked.

"Yes," Proster answered, "But since I came back there has been too many things that need me attention for me to deal with anything to do with Narda."

"Then part of your recovery is going to take some days to deal with your grief," Dr. Kayson said, "Because it will significantly help your recovery."

"Then I will take the next few days to do that," Proster said, "After which I will start into what you have told me to do."

"Then I will see you in three days," Dr. Kayson said as he put his book back in his bag.

"Yes," Proster said. Dr. Kayson got to his feet and walked to the desk. He put the glass bottle and the pendant into his bag. Then he left the study and closed the door behind him. Proster stayed in his chair for several minutes after the door closed.

Finally he stood up. The walking stick was within

reach, but he did not pick it up. Proster took an experimental walk around his desk without using anything for support. His muscles complained a little bit because over the two weeks they had gotten used to the walking stick, but they did not feel the weakness that had been there after the attack. Proster smiled a little. He knew muscle pain and it was not worth the worry his mind had attached to it over the last week. His left hand was still useless, but he hoped Dr. Kayson could suggest some exercises that were not strenuous because most exercises Proster knew would likely do him more damage if he started with them.

Proster left the walking stick where it was as he left his study. The air outside of the room smelled fresher than he remembered. He went up to the second floor balcony and stepped out on to it. It was late evening, so there was no one out there and he could enjoy the cool night air without interruption. It was quiet out as the city was mostly in bed and the guards in the court yard below had already settled into their posts for the night. There were few lit windows in the buildings of the city and slowly more lights were going out.

Across the sky stars were starting to twinkle as they became visible. In the distance there were streaks of green, blue, purple, pink, and a little bit of red on the horizon. It was intermixed streaks which appeared on clear nights in the summer. The first time Proster has seen them they had reminded him of the fireworks displays his father had put on for his mother's birthday. They had been glorious as they lit up the sky with a variety of colours. The flash of color and then the bang of the firecracker. Then more would be set off and the sky would be filled with the lights. But the lights the

Proster could see in the distance from his castle made no sound and he had never found anyone who could tell him what made the lights, or had even seen them up close. When he had first seen them and after questioning some people, Proster had sworn to see the lights up close. However, he had never had the chance to do that kind of traveling and then he did not come out to look at them because he got so busy he forgot about the whole thing.

There were many things he had wanted to do while he had time, which he now doubted he would get to do. If he could get away, which was unlikely, he would be brought back before he reached the lights in the sky. Garrick and Herwin would tell him he was foolish for riding off when his kingdom needed him. But his kingdom would not need him much longer. He needed the space and rest, but there was only one way a king could retire and that was to abdicate. It meant getting his son ready to take the throne, which was going to take a couple years at least. Proster was going to have to start as soon as possible. But not tonight. Tonight, he should find his bed.

There was a sound at the door to the balcony. Proster turned around to look at the castle steward who had stopped to see what was going on.

"I am sorry for interrupting you," the steward said with a bow.

"It is fine," Proster said, "I was just about to come in anyway." Proster went inside. As he passed the steward, he noticed the steward's nose twitch at the smell, which Proster had not noticed until that moment. He took an experimental sniff and realized it was him as he had not bothered to bath in those two weeks of sitting in his study.

"I know it is a little late in the day," Proster said to the steward as the servant closed the balcony doors, "But perhaps you could draw a bath for me."

"It will be ready shortly," the steward said with a slight amount of relief in his voice.

"And have my study aired out," Proster said.

"Yes, Your Majesty," the steward said. He waited briefly to see if there were any more orders. When there were no more, the steward hurried off to do as he was told. Proster gave the steward a five minute head start before meandering up after him.

It was quiet in the castle with most of the servants already gone for the night or in bed. There were torches lighting the hallways so even at night it was easy to navigate the castle. There were few guards on duty inside the castle itself. There were two to three on each gateway out in the court yard and two on the main door to the castle. Two more stood at the door to the throne room as if the royal jewels were in there and needed protecting. Other than those, any guards inside the castle were in a specially set up room on each floor. The room were places where the guards could sleep, or something similar during the night, and yet be able to get to any emergency situation might come up during the night.

So, when Proster reached the top of the main staircase and hear the sound of people moving around below, he did not immediately think it an issue. However, out of habit he checked behind him. The two men, who were tiptoeing through the hallway, were not guards from the kingdom of Proster, but were the two Lord Pardes had brought with him as part of the trade envoy. Proster frowned at this as he was sure he had ordered all members of the trade envoy locked in their rooms at night. He knew Lord Pardes had agreed to that as a precaution for both sides. Lord Pardes did not seem to be the type of man to let his guards out after agreeing to such conditions.

The men had not noticed Proster and were too intent on their destination down a different hallway to see him standing there. Proster was close to calling on his own troops to arrest the men and use them to confront Lord Pardes in the morning, but a shadow separated itself from wall space between torches and followed the men down the hallway. If Proster was not mistaken, the man was named Darwin, who was the son of one of the maids and did odd jobs around the castle. Darwin disappeared in the same direction as the men, but more easily melted into the shadows than the men. As he turned around to head for the bathroom, Proster wondered if Loic had asked Darwin to watch the men, or whether Darwin had taken it upon himself to watch the men and make notes. If it was the second he would have to collect solid evidence of any wrong doing before taking the case to Loic, who would take it seriously either way, but preferred to have useful information over just being told the men were sneaking around. Hopefully the men's purpose would be found out long before any harm would be fall a member of the Kingdom of Proster.

The bath was ready when Proster arrived. It was refreshing and left Proster feeling much better. The steward had laid out clean clothes to go with the towel and had removed the dirty clothes immediately after Proster had gotten into the tub. Feeling relaxed and less under pressure, Proster went to his own room and lay down while trying not to disturb Ruana. She was already asleep because she had not expected him to come up for the night. Proster smiled at the beautiful woman who shared his life.

"I love you," he whispered before kissing her hair. Then he laid his head on his own pillow and closed his eyes.

THREE WEEKS PASS AND MORE
EXCITEMENT TO COME

Hertha had forgotten about the library incident by the next morning and went about her day exactly as she had planned, which was to spend every spare moment with Keften. Keften would have the day off because Lord Pardes would take a couple days off before needing to go over strategy for the next meeting with Proster. Hertha knew having a plan before going into the meeting was pointless, but she did not share the information because Keften was from Grankle and likely to pass the information on to Lord Pardes, who would use it in a meeting with Proster. If Proster found out Lord Pardes had the information then he would go looking for who was leaking it and Hertha was likely to be discovered in her listening post. Then a guard would be posted up there and she would never be allowed to use it again.

With the thoughts of spending the day with Keften and seeing her father at his usual place during breakfast, and memory of the library incident left behind, the world looked brighter and when the world looked brighter, bad things were not important. Proster had appeared to be healthier, even though he looked to have lost some weight. He did not have a walking stick with him, but his left hand remained at his side or hidden from view.

Hertha enjoyed her breakfast before slipping out to meet Keften at their agreed upon hiding spot. She did not worry about security, just discretion. Keften joined her a few minutes after she arrived. They went about their planned day.

Another two weeks went past, but this time Hertha was happier. She spent the same amount of time with Keften as before, but her father was back to his normal self for the most part. His energy lagged a little and his left hand did not work too well, but he was making time for things. And Hertha's visits to the market place with Darwin were their usual fun. There were no other incidents such as what happened that day in the library. Proster did have another meeting with Lord Pardes to discuss the trade agreement, which Hertha listened to. Lord Pardes appeared to believe an agreement was possible and Proster appeared to do the same, but Hertha knew her father was never going to sign such an agreement.

The third week was similar. There was another meeting between Proster and Lord Pardes to discuss the trade agreement. They made no actually progress on it despite talking about various aspects of it for a morning. Lord Pardes was not pushing for them to hurry with it and appeared content with the lack of forward motion. Hertha did not mind as it meant Keften would be around for a while longer, but she did worry about the guards from Grankle and their snooping. Darwin and whoever was helping him did try to keep an eye on them, but occasionally the guards managed to slip away without anyone following them. Darwin was sure several of the others had been spotted by the guards and the guards no longer did anything truly suspicious when they were sure they were being followed. There were no incidents with Hertha and the intruder in the library was long forgotten.

Hertha lay in bed dozing. It was a beautiful day according to the sun shining in the window, but Hertha did not feel like getting up and starting her day. There was nothing she had to do and nothing of interest supposed to be happening. Her bed was comfortable and she was feeling lazy. So, she lay there half asleep, enjoying not doing anything. Her maid had come in several times to check on her and see if she had gotten up, but left after seeing Hertha had not moved. Hertha sometimes heard the door open and close; other times she only heard the door close.

The door closed, causing Hertha to open her eyes. Her maid had come in this time and was standing there as if not certain what to do.

"What is it?" Hertha asked.

"I was wondering if you wanted lunch brought up, or whether you were going to get dressed and eat in the dining room," the maid responded. Hertha looked at the sunshine coming in the window and realized it had shifted to be much higher in the sky.

"I guess I will get up," Hertha said as she slowly moved to sit up. Once she was sitting up in bed, her head started to spin a little and a wave of nausea came over her. Hertha fought the reflex. The maid must have realized what was going on because she grabbed a container and was able to get on to Hertha's lap before the second wave of nausea hit. Hertha could not fight the second wave off and emptied what little was in her stomach into the container. When she was finished, Hertha lay back down with her head over the side of the bed. The maid placed the container under her just in case before leaving the room.

Hertha lay there, but there was no more waves of nausea. Her stomach was upset, but it was hard to tell if it was hungry or ready to give more back. Hertha was not sure where the maid went, but if she came back, Hertha would request some water be brought. Hertha thought about how she had been feeling over the last couple days and what she had eaten, but nothing came to mind as to the cause of this.

How much time had passed since the maid had left, Hertha had no idea, but the door opened again, in stepped the housekeeper followed by the maid. The housekeeper glanced around the room briefly taking it all in at a glance. She strode over to the bed and studied Hertha for a minute. She placed a gentle hand on Hertha's forehead and then cheeks. She checked Hertha's pulse. Hertha did not move.

"You do not have a rise in temperature." the housekeeper said, "How have you been the last few days?"

"Fine," Hertha answered, "I did not even feel like

there was anything wrong until I sat up."

"I see," the housekeeper said with knowing eyes before turning to the maid, "Go get some bread and juice. Tell the cook to make sure it is juice and not his cider."

"Yes, madam," the maid said then hurried off to do what she was told. The housekeeper turned back to Hertha.

"I am going to ask you some questions you may consider private," the housekeeper said, "You answers will determine whether my suspicions are right."

"Ask the questions," Hertha replied.

"Have you been with a man within the last three months?" the housekeeper asked. Hertha hesitated a moment. She really did not want certain people within the castle to find out about her relationship with Keften. The housekeeper's eyes suggested anything said was not open for the world to know.

"Yes," Hertha asked.

"When was the last time you had your monthly bleeding?" the housekeeper asked. Hertha thought about that for several minutes. It was an annoyance, but she had not really paid much attention.

"A month and a half ago," Hertha answered.

"Then it is likely you are with child," the housekeeper said, "The sickness may pass once you eat. Even if it does not, drink as much as you can. You will need to take care of yourself from now on."

Hertha stared at the housekeeper in shock. She could not be pregnant. It was not possible. The housekeeper did not know what she was talking about. This was just a stomach issue and would go away with a little time.

"Rest for now," the housekeeper said. She got

Hertha a wet cloth and put it within Hertha's reach before leaving the room. She closed the door behind her, but Hertha was barely aware she was gone. A few minutes later, the maid came back with the tray from the kitchen. She set the tray on a stool near the bed before pouring some of the juice into the cup and handing it to Hertha. Hertha drank a little without being conscious of the cup or liquid. The maid took the cup back and put it on the tray before offering Hertha some of the bread. Hertha shook her head. The maid put the bread down and picked up the wet cloth. She used it to wipe Hertha's face as if Hertha had a fever and needed it.

The maid sat there by the bed for half an hour offering Hertha things until Hertha requested to be left alone. Then the maid pushed the stool with the tray closer to the bed before leaving the room.

Hertha did not move from where she lay. She did not drink much more and she did not touch the bread. She tried to push the idea the housekeeper brought up out of her head, but it refused to budge. It was like Hertha's body knew there was some truth to it. She could not afford to be with child. Her father would be extremely upset over it and it would be scandalous if the word got out. She was unmarried and without a prospective husband in sight. No one had tried courting her and there was no man who had shown any special interest in her. The few relationships were not with any men who fit within her idea of a husband. It had all been for the fun. None of them had caused this kind of problem. She was going to have to find a solution to this problem before she had to do something like take it to her father and ask for his help.

Hertha remembered when the daughter of a lord was pregnant by one of their servants. It would have been scandalous if the word of the pregnancy had gotten out, but it had not and the girl had gotten rid of the child via a potion brought at the market place. She had been sick for a couple days but then everything was over and her father married her off before anything more could happen. Hertha knew which stall in the market place to buy the potion. He sold all sorts of potions in a stall carefully set up so he never had to change spots. Since it was a little out of the main stream of people he never had it stolen or had to fight for the spot. Hertha had no idea if he owned a shop or anything like that. She had stopped to browse once with Darwin. They had look at the various potions, but had not bought any. They had laughed about some of the potions on the way back to the castle. The man at the stall had been willing to explain or name things and did not try to push them into buying anything. He was likely to be discreet about the transaction, especially since he did not know who she was.

It was an idea, Hertha thought. She started to sit up so she get started, but a wave of nausea forced her to lay back down. If she was going to leave this bed she was going have be feeling better. She picked up the cup and took another sip of the juice. It felt soothing as it went down. She drank a little more before moving on to the bread. It was difficult to get passed the nausea and eat, but once she had gotten a little bit down the rest was easier. So was sitting up. Hertha finished the juice with the bread and felt much better. She could sit up without feeling like she needed a container held for her.

Hertha moved to the edge of the bed and swung her

legs over the side. She sat there a minute or two before putting her feet on the floor. Hertha slowly moved to get to her feet, but was back in a sitting position before she got very far. It was going to be slow going and with being sick, she probably should not go to the market place alone. But she was not sure what Darwin was doing today and she did not want to explain what the potion was for. She might lie and tell him the potion was for an upset stomach, but the few times she had lied to him he had seen through it. Those times had been because she was getting him a present and he had not said anything about the lie, but he still had not liked being lied to even if he had liked the present.

Hertha could not ask Keften to go with her because as of now she could never be alone with him again. The relationship was the cause of this trouble and she did not want it to continue. He might think he had to do the honourable thing and ask for her hand in marriage. Her father might grant it and then she would be stuck. No, she did not want to marry Keften and he must never know about the situation. Maybe she could send him a message of apology about ending the relationship, but she could not see him again.

Hertha moved slowly as she worked toward standing again. The waves of nausea came again, but she swallowed them and just stayed still until they had passed. Doing this she made it to the point where she was standing without too much difficulty. Occasionally she would have to stop and deal with the wave of nausea. Hertha got dressed in the clothing she wore to the market place.

She made her way through the halls. Lunch must have been still in progress because there was no one in sight. Even the kitchen was quiet, though there was sound coming from the hallway that went to the pantry. Hertha exited out the kitchen door. There were still guards in the court yard, but they did not bother her as she headed out the side gate. Hertha headed into the market place.

She found the potion stall without much difficulty, aside from fighting the nausea. The man smiled and waved toward the potions sitting on the table. Hertha looked over the potions on the table. She found the one she was wanted and picked it up.

"Five silver pieces," the man said without looking at which one it was. Hertha took the coins out of her pouch.

"Here," Hertha said as she held out the money. The man took the money, only then did Hertha put the potion into her pouch.

"The instructions are on the back," the man said, "Always follow the directions, or it may kill you."

"Okay," Hertha said with a nod.

"Have a good day," the man said.

"You too," Hertha said before leaving the stall. She headed back up to the castle.

Hertha had not gone very far when she noticed one of the guards from Grankle on the other side of the street. Keeping half an eye on the guard, Hertha ducked into the nearby alley. She watched him from her hiding place. Today there was only one guard, but there was no one following to keep an eye on him. The guard went a little farther down the street, but not out of sight. He went about as far as the potion seller and looked around, but obviously did not see what he was looking for. He started to wander back along the street while still checking around for whatever he was looking for.

Once he was passed, Hertha followed him from a distance. The man did not see her, but she had to be careful to hide when he was checking in her direction. They finally came close to the court yard wall. He was still looking for something. Hertha had ducked into an alley to stay out of sight. The guard stopped at the wall. He looked around again before going to a place just behind a plant where he could see everyone coming or going from the side gate. Hertha watched him for ten minutes before she got tired and decided she needed to get inside. Being careful to stay out of sight from the guard, Hertha moved around to the gate on the other side. She was careful about making sure the other guard was nowhere in sight before going into the court yard. Lunch was over by now and there were more people in the court yard. None of them bothered her as she headed to the closest door. It was the door into the armoury, which fortunately was empty. She went through to the door in the end which went into the castle. After that it was easy to get back to her room.

Another tray was sitting on the table her room having replaced the one that had been brought up this morning. There was a cup of water and another piece of bread. Hertha sat down on the chair in front of the table and pulled out the potion. She ate some of the bread as she read the instructions on the back of the bottle. It said to put three drops in a cup of water and drink the whole cup as fast as possible. Then if there are no symptoms after a day, then to do it again with six drops in the cup of water.

Hertha finished the bread before setting the cup of water closer to her. She opened the potion. It did not have a smell and the liquid was clear. She gently put the three drops into the water. Then she sat there and stared at the cup. She reached out her hand, but stopped short of touching the cup.

She was not sure why, but there was something stopping her from drinking the potion. Hertha was not quite sure what it was. Drinking the potion made sense in so many ways. She did not have to worry about whether she was really pregnant. She did not have to worry about the pregnancy bringing scandal to the royal family. She did not have to worry about hiding the pregnancy from anyone. She did not have to worry about Keften trying to do the honourable thing and asking for her hand in marriage. She did not…

Hertha could not move her hand any closer. The thought that entered her head had nothing to do with logic, or reason. It was her holding the child she had given birth to. She had held a new born baby only once in her whole life and it was like holding a miracle. And she had her own miracle growing inside her. At the time, she wanted to have her own child, but the feeling diminished with some time. However, it never went away completely. She still wanted her own child, but she had hoped she would find a husband first.

If she did not think of it as a baby maybe she could drink the potion and solve her problems. But the image would not leave her head and let her drink the potion in peace. There was an absolute refusal of her mind to get rid of the image and the emotional part of her mind was much stronger today. The rational arguments were not working.

Hertha stood up, which was much easier since she had eaten the other piece of bread. She picked up the cup and took it to the window. Opening the window, Hertha tossed the tainted water out the window. She went back to the table and switched the cup for the potion. She opened the potion and dumped the contents out the window before throwing the bottle after. Then Hertha went to the bed and slumped down on it.

What was she going to do now? She had not been able to get rid of the baby, but she did not know what to do with one. There would be the scandal of her having a child without a husband. Her father was going to be angry at her. And if anyone found out who the father was, she might end up married to Keften. She was going to have to figure out what to do if she was going to avoid all that.

She could find someone away from the city who was willing to take her in for a couple years. It would hide her pregnancy from the people in the city where most of the rumours and gossip would be. She could even pay them for letting her stay out there. But Hertha could not think of anyone with holdings outside the city who she could trust to take her in and not tell her father. Most of them would tell her father because they had been men under him at some point. Those who had not served under him would tell him because it was scandalous to have a pregnant, unmarried daughter.

Running away was not an option. There really was no place to run in the kingdom of Proster and she knew enough of world politics to know she really did not want to leave the kingdom. There was also the knowledge that her disappearance was likely to cause her father more pain and he was just getting better too. She could not do that to her father, even if her pregnancy would leave him disappointed in her.

Finding a husband, marrying the man, and then claiming the baby was his was a possibility. The problem was that Hertha did not know anyone who had enough interest in her to convince them to marry her and she really did not know if she wanted to spend her life with any of them. There were only a few who did not bother with love and were only looking for a good match, but most of them would probably figure out the baby was born too early and accuse her of tricking them. If it was found out that she married to cover up a pregnancy it would be a scandal worse than the pregnancy itself. This kingdom had too much belief in true love.

The church had a branch of women who took care of orphans and sick. They had a special title, which Hertha could not remember. They willing took anyone into their ranks and were willing to overlook the pregnancy as long as when she joined their ranks she took a vow of celibacy. However, Hertha could not see herself in a position such as that, or leaving her current lifestyle behind for one set of clothes and a bare cell. That was especially true if she wanted to keep the child. Her faith in God was also somewhat limited these days, even though she still went with her mother to church every Sunday. There was not even a saint she sent her prayers to.

Or Hertha could just face the scandal of being an unmarried and pregnant, tell her father and accept his anger. She would not tell anyone who the father was. If Keften showed up to claim his child she would tell him she was not sure it was his, she had other lovers at the time and because of that she could not let him do the honourable thing. She would give birth alone and raise the child the same way. She would likely have to find a house in the city to move into and out of the castle, but she would not have to go too far. She could do it that way, but not until it was obvious she was carrying a child. Yes, only then would she admit to her condition. Hertha's eyes drifted closed and she fell asleep.

The sound of the maid coming in to take the tray barely registered to Hertha. The housekeeper coming in to check on her was just another noise she did not notice. The guard who was ordered to stand guard at her door and had loud armour was just another sound causing her to twitch in her sleep, but did not wake her up. There were normal everyday noises from outside the window, which though occasionally had bothered her before, did not bother her right now. She slept right through supper and the night following. The housekeeper sent up a tray of food just in case Hertha woke up hungry, but the maid delivered it to the same response as everything else got. However, the housekeeper ordered the maid not to return the tray but leave it there for the night, just in case.

The sunlight was starting into the sky when Hertha finally woke up. The small amount of light in the room came from the window and the rest came from a candle burning down low near her bed. It had been left lit by the housekeeper on her last check of the night. Hertha sat up and looked around. Her room looked the same, but a tray of food sat on the table. She was feeling queasy, but not as bad as the day before. She was a little cold.

Hertha got out of bed and closed the window before wrapping herself in a blanket and sitting down at the table. She ate small amounts of the cold foods off the tray as she stared into space. She had made several decisions about her future and she was not sure any of them were right.

When she was finished as much of the food as she thought she could handle, Hertha got herself dressed. The maid was likely to be still asleep and not be up for another hour or two. Hertha had gotten used to doing her own hair and dressing without help so it was not an issue for her. When she was dressed, Hertha left her room and headed to the library. She had left the book she had been reading on the shelf rather than take it with her and now she wanted to finish it.

The library was quiet at this time of the morning. Zebulon would not arrive until after breakfast and very few other people used it. Her father had been known to show up in the library at this time of day, but it usually was because he had been up all night dealing with some matter which required research. Hertha doubted he was awake today because there was nothing happening in the kingdom which required such research at the moment.

Hertha did not pause upon entering the library, but headed straight for the shelf she wanted. Only when she was standing there with her hand on the book did she hear the sound of someone else being in the library. She froze and listened. The person was on the left side of the library and shifting their feet in front of the encyclopedia section. As Hertha listened they did not move from the section, just shifted back and forth on their feet. They did not seem to be trying to do anything silently, but the memory of the incident from three weeks ago came back to Hertha as she stood there listening. She was scared to move, but the person must have heard her and did not come looking for her or anything like that.

Hertha slowly slipped the book off the shelf and concentrated on moving as quietly as possible back toward the door. She was hoping not to disturb the other person and merely take the book back to her room unseen. But she had not heard the other person moving away from the encyclopedia section until they rounded the shelf coming toward the door, which was where Hertha was headed. Hertha saw it was Lord Pardes and he had one of the encyclopaedias open in his hands. He was dressed in well-worn trousers and shirt with reading glasses perched on the end of his nose, which was a lot different than he looked when he met with her father to discuss the trade agreement. He looked as surprised to see her as she was to see him.

"Um," Lord Pardes coughed slightly, "Good morning." He seemed uncomfortable as they both stood there.

"Good morning," Hertha responded out of politeness, "I did not expect anyone else in the library at this early in the morning."

"I, um, have been visiting to get some reading material for the day," Lord Pardes said.

"It looks like fairly heavy reading," Hertha said.

"I have read most of the rest of the set," Lord Pardes said, "And figured I would just read the next one." Hertha realized he was not bragging, but just telling her the facts. His face also opened up a bit at the reference to the book.

"I never thought about reading the whole volume of an encyclopedia before," Hertha said, "Just looking up information from them as necessary."

"Normal I would only use them for looking up specific information too," Lord Pardes said, "But I have found so much interesting information in this set of encyclopaedias that I started to just read it. It is quite fascinating. What have you picked up to read?"

"A book of short tales," Hertha held it up.

"Hadden Grimes," Lord Pardes read off the cover, "He is very good at telling tales. I heard his tales as a child and then I had not read anything from him for a long time until I received a copy of one of his books. As first I thought it was children's tales and silly to read it as an adult, but once I got into them I found them to be very much more enjoyable as an adult than I ever did as a child."

"My father used to read them to me," Hertha said, "And as soon as I could read on my own, I went through the book several times. I like it more every time I read through it. My favourite is The Hungry Bear."

"I always liked the story about the tea cup," Lord Pardes said, "But I have only ever found it in the one volume and not in any of the others."

"I do not recall ever reading one about a tea cup," Hertha said.

"I have only found it in the one book myself," Lord Pardes said, "I have the book with me. If you would like I can lend it to you to read. It contains many stories I have never found in any other volume of tales."

"I would like that," Hertha said, "I have read this book so many times. It is a very good read, but I would love to read different tales by Hadden Grimes."

"We can get it now," Lord Pardes said as he stuck

his finger in the encyclopedia to mark his place before closing the book around it and starting for the door, "There is another story in there called The House with Two Doors that is really good too." Lord Pardes held the door open for Hertha. She stepped out into the hallway and he closed the door before heading down the hallway opposite from the way Hertha had come. She followed him.

Lord Pardes' suite of rooms was not very far down the hallway. He went inside while Hertha waited in the hallway. It took a few minutes before Lord Pardes came back out with the book.

"Here," Lord Pardes said as he offered the book to Hertha. She took the book from him.

"Thank you," Hertha said. Lord Pardes stood there as if he was not sure what to say.

"I will get it back to you as soon as possible," Hertha said.

"Okay," Lord Pardes said, "I hope you enjoy it."

"Thank you," Hertha said. She turned and headed back to her own room. She heard the door close shortly after she had turned around.

Hertha went back to her room and curled up in her bed with the Hadden Grimes book Lord Pardes had loaned her. When her maid arrived, Hertha was so involved in the book she did not even notice the maid was there. The maid noted Hertha was already dressed, so she just took the tray away. The maid brought a tray of breakfast and set it near the bed. Between stories Hertha stopped for a few minutes to eat a little bit of breakfast, but she did not eat anywhere close to everything on the tray because her stomach would not allow her eat too much.

Hertha was about half way through the book when she came to a story called, The Queen's Tea Cup. Hertha took a short break to have a drink and get more comfortable. Then she started to read the story.

Once upon a time in a far-away kingdom there lived a king and queen, who were happy. They lived in a small kingdom with friendly neighbours. There were very few problems within the kingdom. The citizens were happy and healthy. The royal couple lived in a simple life in a small palace, which had enough room for them to live comfortably along with their servants. They had seven servants. There was the steward named Henry, a housekeeper named Sophia, a maid named Isa, a man's man named Jegar, a cook named Melody, a stable master named Travers, and a boy to do odd jobs named Drew.

It was one day in late October and Melody was in the kitchen getting things ready for tea time. Tea time was the queen's favourite time of day and all the servants worked hard to make as pleasant and wonderful as possible. There were specific dishes that were the queen's favourites. The treats served were the queen's favourites and were only ever served at tea time. The tea was especially purchased and shipped in for tea time. It was the kingdom's only extravagance.

That day the king and queen were in town to open a new town hall recently built and would be back for tea time. The rest of the servants were busy with their own jobs in other parts of the palace. Melody had the treats already baked and cooling. She put water in the kettle and left it on the stove to boil. She switched her attention to gathering the dishes.

She started by taking the tray down from the cupboard and setting it on the counter. Next was the tea pot, which was set in its proper place before the cream and sugar dishes were brought down. Both were filled before being set on the tray. Then there was the necessary silverware, which were checked over to make sure they were shining and those pieces that were not had to be wiped until they did. They were set in their place on the tray. The small plates were brought out and set on the tray. Then Melody reached up for the two tea cups, which were always used to serve the tea at tea time.

The king had a blue cup with white and gold lines at the top of the cup and matching saucer. The queen's cup was a bright yellow with purple flowers at intervals around the outside. There was also a beautifully painted flower at the bottom of the cup. This cup had a saucer to match as well. And they were always kept in the same place on the second shelf in the cupboard with the tray and tea pot.

Melody's left hand connected with the blue cup, but her right hand did not connect with anything. This caused her to look up. The blue cup was indeed there, but the yellow cup was gone. Melody gasped and let go of the blue cup. She started to search the kitchen for the yellow cup in case it had been put away in the wrong place. She went through every cupboard, every cabinet, every drawer, the wash pile, the drying pile, and the garbage area. The cup was nowhere to be found. Melody was shocked and stunned at the disappearance of the yellow tea cup. The queen's yellow tea cup. It was gone and there was no trace of it. Melody collapsed in the middle of the kitchen and started to cry.

Henry heard some crying and followed the sound to Melody in the kitchen. He surveyed the displaced dishes, the open drawers, and the sobbing woman on the floor.

"What is going on?" Henry asked.

"It is gone!" Melody answered between sobs.

"What is gone?" Henry asked.

"The queen's yellow tea cup," Melody answered, "I looked everywhere and it is gone."

"Oh dear! Perhaps it has been misplaced," Henry said, "Someone might have accidently used it and taken it to another room. It is just forgotten and not brought back. We can still find it, wash it, and it will be ready when the king and queen arrive."

"Do you think so?" Melody asked looking up at him with teary eyes.

"Come on," Henry said, "Let us go look." Henry offered Melody a hand up and pulled her to her feet. They left the kitchen with Melody following Henry.

Henry led the way to the next room, which they searched from top to bottom without finding the queen's yellow tea cup. They continued moving from room, searching each very carefully. They reached the main hall of the palace, where Sophia was busy sweeping the floor. She looked up at Henry and Melody. She noticed Melody's tear streaked face and Henry's worried eyes.

"What is wrong?" Sophia asked stopping her sweeping.

"The queen's yellow tea cup is missing," Melody said with a sniffle.

"We have been searching the palace room by room

*in hopes it was misplaced and forgotten somewhere,"
Henry said.*

*"I will help you," Sophia said setting her broom to
one side. The three of them proceeded to search the
main hall top to bottom. When they finished the main
hall, the three moved on to the next room which they
searched in the same way. They continued moving
room to room, searching from top to bottom, leaving
nothing unsearched.*

*They reached the queen's bedroom where Isa was
busy setting out the outfit the queen was going wear for
tea. She looked up as Henry, Melody, and Sophia
entered the room. Isa noticed the worried eye, the tear
streaks, and the concerned frown.*

"What is wrong?" Isa asked.

*"The queen's yellow tea cup is missing," Melody
answered.*

*"We have been searching the palace room to room
in hopes it was misplaced and forgotten somewhere,"
Henry said.*

*"We must find it before the king and queen return,"
Sophia said.*

*"I will help you," Isa said as she put down the piece
of clothing she was holding. The four of them started to
search the room. When they had finished the four of
them moved on to the next room. They searched it top
to bottom. Once they were finished, they moved on to
the next room and did the same.*

*Henry, Melody, Sophia, and Isa came to the king's
bedroom and stepped inside. Jegar looked up at them
from his polishing of the king's shoes .He saw Henry's
worried eyes, Melody's tear stained face, Sophia's
concerned frown, and Isa's clasping hands.*

"What is wrong?" Jegar asked.

"The queen's yellow tea cup is missing," Melody answered.

"We have been searching the palace room to room in hopes it was misplaced and forgotten somewhere," Henry said.

"We must find it before the king and queen return," Sophia said.

"They will be back in a short amount of time," Isa said.

"I will help you," Jegar said as he put down the shoes and got to his feet. They searched the room. When they finished searching the room, they moved on to the next one. They continued to search the palace room to room top to bottom. They reached the top tower of the palace without finding the queen's yellow tea cup. When they did they stood and looked at each other to try and figure out what to do next.

"Perhaps we should check the stable," Henry said, "It is the last place the queen's yellow tea cup could be."

"Let us go and check," Sophia said.

The five of them headed down to the bottom level and out back to where the stable was. Travers and Drew were in the stable and looked up when the five entered. Travers saw the worried eyes, tear streaks, concerned frown, clasping hands, and gnawed lip.

"What is wrong?" Travers asked.

"The queen's yellow tea cup is missing," Melody answered.

"We have been searching the palace room to room in hopes it was misplaced and forgotten somewhere," Henry said.

"We must find it before the king and queen return," Sophia said.

"They will be back in a short amount of time," Isa said.

"We could not find it anywhere in the palace," Jegar said.

"We need to keep searching then," Travers said getting to his feet.

"I know where it is," Drew said.

Everyone turned to Drew with wide eyes and open mouths.

"Where is it?" Travers asked.

"I found a kitten out in the rain last night," Drew said, *"It was mewing something awful and I took it in. I dried it off and then went looking for something to put some milk in. I did not realize it was the queen's tea cup."*

"Where is it now?" Henry asked, *"Perhaps it can still be washed and set on the table."*

"I will go get it," Drew said. He headed up into the loft of the stable. He came back with the tea cup in his hand. The yellow tea cup was no longer yellow. It was covered in dirt and horse manure. A small kitten followed Drew down from the loft and started circling Drew's legs. It meowed and looked up at the cup as if asking for the cup to be refilled.

"I am sorry," Drew said, *"I did not realize what cup I was using."*

"We will have to find the queen a different cup," Melody said as she looked down at the kitten. She found she could not take the cup away from the cute creature. She stooped down to pet the kitten on its head before straightening up and heading back inside.

In the kitchen there was a large mess because she had not put things away when she was searching. The kettle was boiling and the treats had cooled. The other servants came back into the palace as well. Each room was in the same type of mess as the kitchen. Each servant took the rooms of which they were responsible for and hurriedly cleaned them as fast as possible to get it done before the king and queen arrived home.

Everything was ready when the king and queen arrived back at the palace. They went up to their rooms where Isa and Jegar helped them change clothes. Then the king and queen took their seats on the balcony where the table was set out for them to have tea. Melody was not sure how to explain what happened to the queen's yellow tea cup, but decided to tell the truth when asked about it.

The tray was set down on the table and the queen served the king and then herself. They each had some treats off the plate while they enjoyed the sun of the afternoon. The queen never asked what happened to her yellow tea cup and when Melody went back to the kitchen she took some cream out to fill the kitten's yellow tea cup.

Hertha looked up at the sound of her room door opening. She looked up to see her maid come in. The maid took the tray and left the room again. Hertha's eyes went back to the book in her hand. She smiled at it. The Queen's Tea Cup was a good story just as Lord Pardes had said. She flipped to the next story. It was called The House with Two Doors. Hertha shifted her position to get comfortable again and then went back to reading.

Once upon a time in a small town called Hefton there lived a tailor. His name was Tate and his shop was the last building before the road headed into the forest which surrounded the small town. Tate was a cheery individual who did good work, but was not known for his brains. He rarely went out, but when he did he practically skipped rather than walk. He had stick like arms and legs with a body to match. He had glasses which were always sliding down his nose and seemed like they were going to slide right off if he did not push them up every minute or so. His clothing fit perfectly, but the hat he wore was floppy and fell on the top of his glasses making them slide down farther. His shoes were also a size too big and made many wonder how he managed to skip without falling on his nose. Some of the people in the small town would make fun of him, but he just smiled and continued on his way. His life was happy in his small house.

One day in the heat of a late summer, a spark came too near Tate's small house. The wood was as dry as the grass Tate never got around to cutting and the wall went up in flame. There was no time to react. It spread to the roof and the other walls just as quickly. Tate's neighbours hurried with their buckets to try and put out the fire, but soon their attention had to shift to their own houses as the sparks from Tate's house were setting fires as far as the wind could scatter them. In an hour, the humble building that had been Tate's home was now a pile of ash. The rest of the fires were put out without too much damage to his neighbours.

During the fire Tate had been in the market place getting his usual supplies. When he arrived back from his errands he found chaos around his house as people worked to put out the last embers to prevent any other fires from springing up. Tate's smile dimmed for the first time anyone could remember as he sat down on a nearby crate and looked at the place where his house had been. But there was nothing anyone could do that day as night was falling when the last of the embers had been thoroughly covered in water and stomped out.

Tate was offered supper, which he took, and a bed for the night, which he turned down. The neighbours watched out their windows as Tate proceeded to use a borrowed broom and sweep the ashes that had been his house into a pile. He collected them up and scattered them over a patch of green clover which grew behind where his house had been. The clover had been trampled during the chaos of putting out fires, but was already starting to straighten back up. He gently scattered the ashes before taking a bucket of water and watering the clover.

When he was finished, Tate took a blanket loaned to him and wrapped himself in it before lying down on the freshly cleared ground. The neighbours watched as he fell asleep. They shook their heads before closing their windows and heading toward their comfortable beds.

In the morning, some of the town carpenters showed up at Tate's plot of ground with offers to help Tate rebuild his house. Tate accepted their help on the condition they make it exactly as he specified. Thinking Tate would have normal requests, the carpenters accepted the condition as well as Tate's agreed amount he could pay.

The carpenters brought the building materials to the spot and one was picked out to lead the whole team and *then they all turned to Tate for a discussion on what he wanted built. He explained he wanted three separate rooms with the workshop at the front and the bedroom and kitchen at the back. And the front door had to be exactly in the middle of the front and the back door exactly in line with the front door. The wall separated the workshop from the rooms had to have a door shaped opening matching with the front and back door. One should be able to look through the opening for the front door and see all the way to the clover patch in the back without anything in the way.*

The carpenters gave Tate strange looks, but he stood firm and they had already agreed to it. So, they started working on building Tate a house. With all the carpenters working as a team they managed to get the floor done as well as two of the walls before night fell. Once again Tate was offered supper, which he accepted, and a place to sleep, which he refused. He surveyed the wok so far and nodded in approval. Then he wrapped himself in the blanket and lay down on the newly made floor.

In the morning, the carpenters came back to work on the house. They put in the second two walls and the roof. On the third day they came back to finish the inside of the house. They build the walls separating the kitchen, bedroom, and workshop. They also built Tate a work table, a bed, and a couple chairs. When everything was finished, Tate paid them what he said he could and they split it among themselves.

Tate surveyed his house and found it completely to his satisfaction, especially the two doors which were exactly the same place in the front as well as the back. He went and bought what he could with the money he had left, so that this new house would feel like home. He went back to work in his new workshop and life went on. Slowly he bought the rest of what he needed to live and he contributed a little more to the group of carpenters who had helped him build the house.

A few years passed and every year there was speculation as to why Tate needed two doors, one in the front and one in back with them matching up exactly. His neighbours reported Tate only ever used the front door, even when going out to do something at the back on his house. The back door was never opened and never used. Some people asked the carpenters, who just shrugged and said they only built it, they did not explain it. It was once again something to laugh at Tate for as he passed them in the market place doing his funny skip in too big shoes. He just smiled and bought what needed before going back to his new home.

Another hot summer arrived and the grass was once again dry. Tate did not go out as much this summer, only brief trips to the market place and when then people noticed he was in a hurry to get back. The people shrugged it off as him worrying his house might catch on fire while he was gone. They understood the reasoning. They might have such a worry themselves would they ever be in the same position.

One night that summer, one of Tate's neighbours could not sleep so he decided to go for a short walk to cool down and find some way of going back to sleep. He headed for the edge of the forest and was only going that far before coming back. He passed Tate's house and saw the front door was open, so he looked inside to see if everything was okay. He found himself looking straight through the house to the patch of green *clover which was surrounded by grass dead from too much heat and not enough water. The neighbour thought it weird. Tate was nowhere to be seen, but did not seem to be in danger so the neighbour walked on. The house was the same when he passed it again to get back to his own. But when the neighbour went passed the day after, the doors were closed. The neighbour was curious, so he kept an eye on Tate's house during the day and many times at night. The doors were closed during the day unless Tate opened the front one, but more nights than not both doors stood open.*

Later that month the neighbour was awake early in the morning to prepare for his day of work. He stepped outside to get some water and heard some noise coming from Tate's house. He looked over and saw Tate stomping out sparks outside his back door, which was open. The sparks were not being given enough time to light anything on fire because Tate was stomping them out so fast. The neighbour realized the noise was Tate shouting and was surprised it had not woken anyone up. Then what Tate was yelling sunk in and surprised the neighbour.

"Quit your nonsense," Tate was shouting, "You got your door to play ball. You do not need to play with them sparks."

The neighbour could not see who or what Tate was shouting at, but was surprised to see the tailor angry. He watched Tate for several minutes. Tate finished stamping out the sparks and poured a bucket of water over the area. Then Tate went into his house and closed the back door. The neighbour shook his head at Tate's behaviour and got his water before going back inside.

Hertha stretched and went on to read the next story. She finished the book, set it to one side, ate a little more from the tray the maid had set near the bed, and then went to sleep.

Hertha woke to the maid coming into her room. The maid took the tray and left. Hertha glanced at the window and noticed that by the sun it was morning. She got out of bed despite the waves of nausea. She changed from yesterday's clothes into something clean. She did her own hair rather than wait for the maid to come back. Then she tucked the book into her pocket and left her bedroom. She went down to the library and went inside. She checked it over, but Lord Pardes was not there. Likely he had been and gone already.

With a sigh, Hertha headed for the dining room. It was mostly full with people waiting for breakfast to be served. Hertha sat down at her usual table. She noticed Zebulon was already at his table, but her parents were not there yet. The table which the group from Grankle sat was still empty. Slowly more people came into the dining room. The group from Grankle came in altogether. Keften was with them as were the two guards. Hertha avoided looking at Keften. A few minutes later Proster and Ruana came into the dining room together and sat at the raised table. Shortly after breakfast was served.

Hertha ate what little she could before she was worried it might come back on her. Then she left the dining room. She was the first one to leave, so Hertha went up to Lord Pardes suite. She made sure she had the book in her hand before she knocked on the door. A minute passed before she could hear movement from the other side. Another minute past before the door opened. Lord Pardes stood there looking like he had the morning before in the library.

"Hello," Lord Pardes said.

"I brought your book back," Hertha said holding it out to him, "I finished reading it yesterday."

"What did you think of it?" Lord Pardes asked taking the book.

"I really liked it," Hertha answered, "The Queen's Tea Cup was a good story, but I did not like The House with Two Doors as much."

"It does have an unfinished quality to it," Lord Pardes said, "But I enjoy the first part of it."

"The first part as okay," Hertha said, "But my favourite tale will always be the Prince and the Miller's Daughters."

"I do not think I have read that story," Lord Pardes said, "I may have to borrow your book of Hadden Grimes' tales."

"It is not in that book," Hertha said, "It came from a volume which went missing years ago."

"That is a pity," Lord Pardes said, "I would have liked to read it."

"Did you move on to the next encyclopaedia in the set?" Hertha asked.

"Not quite yet," Lord Pardes answered, "But probably by the end of today. I read fast, but not that fast."

"The only person in the castle who has read all the way through those encyclopaedias is Zebulon," Hertha said, "I think he has read most of the books in the library. He might be able to talk to you about them."

"I have been in there when he is reading," Lord Pardes said, "The books he is currently reading are outside my interest. I am reading more general knowledge books and the ones he has been reading have been on very specific topics. His are religion, politics, and a couple on the human condition. I have read my share of books on those topics and find I do better when I read a larger range."

"To be truthful, I have never paid much attention to what he reads," Hertha said, "But he spends enough time in the library to have read most of the books in there. I have been very specific in my reading with most of it being fiction over knowledge."

"Sometimes it is the better thing to read," Lord Pardes said, "I mix it with knowledge because I have always craved the information."

"Maybe the amount of knowledge you have acquired is why the King of Grankle chose you to come and negotiate the trade agreement," Hertha said. Lord Pardes looked slightly embarrassed at the mention of the trade agreement.

"Actually, I requested the job of negotiating the trade agreement," Lord Pardes admitted shyly.

"Why?" Hertha asked.

"Because I hoped to get access to the castle library," Lord Pardes answered, "There are several volumes in this library that cannot be found in any other."

"So, you do not mind that the negotiations are taking so long," Hertha said with a smile a shake of her head, "Most of the other representatives from Grankle have been in a hurry to secure a trade agreement, or a treaty, to the point of being pushy."

"From looking at the notes of the previous

representatives they all have come to the Kingdom of Proster with the belief a trade agreement or treaty should be an easy proposition," Lord Pardes said, "Even men I have met and thought to be intelligent are in complete disbelief when they are thrown out after pushing their way into court. I tried to avoid the pushy behaviour in hopes King Proster would allow me to stay long enough I could read some of the books I wanted. But my expectations have been more than met with his willingness to talk over a trade agreement over the period of weeks. "

"I hope you are not too disappointed if you leave without a trade agreement set," Hertha said, "My father has had a long history of hatred toward Grankle."

"I do not care about the trade agreement," Lord Pardes said, "I do not expect King Proster to do anything about the trade agreement. I am surprised he has allowed the talk to get this far. All I am doing is reading books from the library, because this was the only way I could think of which would get me anywhere close to it."

"He may have let you stay if you had just come out and said you were interested in reading books from the library," Hertha said.

"True," Lord Pardes said, "But the King of Grankle would have gotten upset with me for not obeying orders to stay out of the Kingdom of Proster and there is also a travel ban between the two kingdoms unless on official business. It is just easier this way."

"What happens if you return to Grankle without a trade agreement?" Hertha asked.

"I write a report for the next person who the King of Grankle will send as a representative," Lord Pardes said, "And the King of Grankle will be disappointed in me. Other than that not much is going to happen. If luck is with me, I will not be in Grankle very long after I finish here."

"Why is that?" Hertha asked.

"I sent a request to study under one of the teachers at the Great Library," Lord Pardes said, "I am expecting response soon as to whether I can go or not. Many scholars request such an honour, but only a few are accepted."

"What about your family and title?" Hertha asked.

"My family is okay with it and happy for me if I am accepted," Lord Pardes answered, "The family title has been passed on to my younger brother. He has always been interested in the business of running the estate and he has three children with his wife. It works out much better for everyone for him to have the title and the estate while I have the freedom to continue my studies."

"That makes everything work out nicely," Hertha said.

The sound of footsteps could be heard coming down the hall. Most likely it was the group coming back from breakfast. Hertha's immediate thought was Keften might be among them and she should leave before the group arrived, but she did not want to end the conversation too abruptly in an effort not to seem rude because she had actually enjoyed talking to Lord Pardes. However Lord Pardes also appeared to not want anyone to see them talking as his behaviour changed slightly.

"I should get back to my reading if I am to get the encyclopaedia finished today," Lord Pardes said.

"Thank you for loaning me the book," Hertha said.

"I am glad you enjoyed it," Lord Pardes said, "Perhaps at some point you can tell me the story of the Prince and the Miller's daughters."

"Perhaps," Hertha said with a slight smile. She turned and headed down the hallway. This time it was a minute after she turned before she heard the door close.

Hertha passed the library before the group from Grankle passed her. She noticed Keften was not among them and wondered whether he was looking for her. Hertha shook that thought out of her head. She could not afford to meet with Keften, or to be left alone with him. Instead she headed out to the garden to get some fresh air.

It was quiet in the garden. The two gardeners were working in a back corner and there was no one else out there. Hertha wandered some of the paths looking at the variety of flowers in bloom and appreciating the beauty of nature. She reached the centre of garden and sat down on the bench in an area of cobblestones. It faced the castle, but the other direction was just the castle wall. Aside from the trees growing along the wall the view was not really much different.

Hertha pushed away all the thoughts trying to fill her head and just let the wonder of nature surround her. There was the fresh air, the smell of the flowers and the chirping of the birds from the trees. It was pleasant to just sit in contentment. Hertha did not remember the last time she had just sat and enjoyed something like sitting outside. She had never spent much time in the garden, but remembered her mother complaining about Narda wandering out to the garden and not coming in when called. Hertha now understood why Narda liked it out here and why it was difficult to get her to come back inside.

The sound of a door opening and movement near the castle drew Hertha out of her own thoughts. She looked over to see Keften and one of the female servants from the castle exit the door and head into the closest shed. Hertha could see the smile on the maid's face that would have mirrored her own if it had been a few days ago. Between the distance and their attention just for each other, they did not notice Hertha sitting on the bench. They disappeared into the shed and the door closed behind them.

Hertha felt the tears in her eyes, the dry throat, and the pain in her abdomen. She focused on holding them back. After all she was the one who stopped seeing him without even telling him. She had been the one worried he would want to do the honourable thing. She really should not be surprised he had moved on, or that he had other lovers. He was a good looking man after all. Hertha swallowed her tears and what was left of her feelings. They were wasted on Keften and she knew that before the relationship had started.

Hertha pushed thoughts of Keften away. He was not worth the tears. Memories of the first day in the market place came back to Hertha. Watching Lord Pardes ride through the market place with Keften riding behind him. She had thought Lord Pardes would be a stuck up, arrogant person and Keften would be the likeable one. It turned out Lord Pardes was the likeable person and Keften was the jerk. Though Hertha could not see herself as anything more than friends with Lord Pardes, who had not so far mention whether he was married or not. He had mentioned his brother's wife and it was not unreasonable that if he were married his wife would stay at home rather than travel with him. After all he hoped he would get to stay a while, but did not know for sure whether he would. Also, if he was spending all his time reading books from the library, she would probably get bored. But then if Lord Pardes had requested to be a scholar at the Great Library, then she is probably used to him being busy with reading and had some hobbies of her own.

It was fifteen minutes later that Keften and the servant came out of the shed. She was still straightening her clothing. They went back inside the castle and the door closed behind them. Hertha took a deep breath and closed her eyes. She concentrated on the smell of flowers, the light breeze going passed her, and the chirping of the birds. It relaxed her and brought her back to her mindset before she had seen Keften and the servant.

It was not until her stomach growled that she opened her eyes. The sun had moved from being at an angle to just about overhead. Hertha got up and headed back along the path. She walked at a leisurely pace to continue enjoy the garden. When she reached the door, Hertha went inside. She went directly to the dining room. There were other people already waiting for lunch. She sat down at her usual spot and waited. Slowly more people arrived, but it was only after Proster and Ruana arrived that lunch was served.

After lunch Hertha went up to her room and sat down on the chair with the Hadden Grimes' book. She started at the first story and spent all afternoon reading the rest of it.

Proster lay on the couch in his study and stared up at

the ceiling. Thane stood inside the door of the study. It was quiet in the study with only the sounds of breathing. It was early evening. A knock came at the door and Thane opened it, but Proster did not move at all. Dr. Kayson entered the study and looked around. Thane closed the door and stepped back in front of it. Dr. Kayson glanced at Thane.

"I found him in the hallway outside the study," Thane answered, "He had collapsed but was still conscious. I made sure he could breathe before bringing him in here and having him lie down on the couch."

"Proster?" Dr. Kayson said once he was beside the couch. Proster looked at him and mouthed something. It looked like he tried reaching up with his left hand, but it would not move. Dr. Kayson looked him over and then pulled a chair over. Taking Proster's left hand, Dr. Kayson looked over it before poking and prodding. The muscles Proster had been building up felt like they had disappeared in less than a day. Proster's eyes had drifted back to the ceiling as if he had forgotten Dr. Kayson was there.

"Proster," Dr. Kayson said. Proster brought his eyes back to Dr. Kayson.

"You were relaxing, getting sleep, exercise, drinking less, and eating better?" Dr. Kayson asked. Proster nodded and tried to say something, but no sound came out. Dr. Kayson could not even tell what he was trying to say by reading his lips.

"You are getting worse," Dr. Kayson said, "Though by following my suggestion you are not dying at the same rate as before, but you are just going to get worse. At this rate you have six months to a year before you are incapacitated. From there it is a sad and painful death. Rarely have I seen anyone go from healthy to sick so quickly."

Proster opened his mouth and his lips moved slowly as if he was trying to ask a question with the hope the Dr. Kayson could read his lips. Dr. Kayson shook his head because he did not understand.

"He asked if there is anything more he could do to lessen the symptoms," Thane said. Dr. Kayson looked up at Thane, who was still standing in front of the door, and then glanced back at Proster. Proster nodded.

"Prayer?" Dr. Kayson said with a shrug, "What you are doing already is everything medicine knows helps with your condition. I don't know what else to suggest." Proster nodded slightly and closed his eyes. Dr. Kayson made sure that Proster was breathing properly before getting to his feet.

"Keep an eye on him," Dr. Kayson said, "And give him a drink of water when he wakes up."

Thane nodded. Dr. Kayson double checked Proster before leaving the room. Thane closed the door behind Dr. Kayson and then locked it behind him. Thane listened to Proster breath for several minutes as Proster slipped into a deeper sleep. He waited a few minutes more before going over and sitting down in the chair Dr. Kayson had pulled over to the couch. Thane took Proster's left hand and placed the medallion of St. Durward in the palm. He bent the fingers over it and bowed his head.

"St. Durward, help this soul heal from his illness," Thane whispered, "Yes, he is a patron of St. Ingram, but St. Ingram seems to no longer be with him. Please help him heal enough to finish what he needs to finish. He needs his health and wisdom to get through this time. St. Durward, I ask this of you." Thane stayed in that position, though he was quiet.

Pain disappeared from Proster's face and his left hand gripped the medallion briefly before letting go. Thane left out a breath with a thank you before taking the medallion and putting it back around his neck. Then Thane put the chair back in its proper place before going back to standing by the door.

Proster opened his eyes and looked up at the ceiling. He was lying on the couch in his study. He did not try to sit up, but he did start coughing. A moment later Thane held out a cup of water. Proster took the cup and took a drink. It helped ease the dryness of his throat and Thane took the cup back when Proster handed it to him. A few minute went past before Proster sat up. He felt slightly better, but was still weak.

"How late is it?" Proster asked.

"A couple hours past when you have been turning in," Thane answered.

"I should get to bed," Proster said as he used both hands to push himself off the couch. He was obviously weak, but he could move on his own.

Thane opened the door and let Proster exit the room ahead of him. Poster led the way through the hallways, which were quiet due to everyone else being in bed. They had just gotten up to the top of the stairs when they heard the sound of footsteps from below. Both turned to see the guards from Grankle moving down the hallway below. Thane's eyes narrowed but he did not move. They stood silently and watched. Once the guards had disappeared down the hallway the shadow of the stable master's son followed them. Once he had disappeared, they turned back around.

"Think Loic knows?" Thane asked in a whispered.

"I doubt it," Proster answered in the same volume, "But I am sure he will."

"Should one of us be there when they tell him so we can confirm what they tell him?" Than asked.

"Hopefully they will have enough evidence to convince him," Proster said.

They continued down the hallway to Proster's bedroom. Proster went inside while Thane took up his position outside the door.

FRIENDSHIP CREATED, BUT PROBLEMS ON HORIZON

Hertha put the Hadden Grimes book on the table beside the chair she had picked in the main area of the library. Then she sat down in the chair. It was so early in the morning the sun had not risen yet, but the sky was light. It was not enough light to read by, but it was enough to see by. She had woken up a little past midnight and had not been able to get back to sleep because she kept throwing up everything she had eaten the day before. It was only after she had emptied her stomach did she feel up to going to the library and finding a different book to read. However reaching the library, she was forced to sit down and rest to avoid more stomach acid coming up. She sat there and waited for the nausea to abate.

Hertha was still sitting there when the sun came up and the library door opened. She looked up to see Lord

Pardes enter the library. Lord Pardes smiled and nodded to Hertha before heading toward the encyclopaedia section with the volume he had borrowed in his hand. When he came back out he had the next volume of the encyclopaedia in his hand. He sat down in the chair across from Hertha.

"On to the next volume?" Hertha asked.

"One of the last three in the set," Lord Pardes answered.

"Then what are you going to read?" Hertha asked.

"The Hadden Grimes book," Lord Pardes answered, "I am not sure what I will read after that. There were a few books I had hoped to read and thought were supposed to be here, but I have not been able to find them."

"They could be in my father's study," Hertha said, "He keeps books he did not want us to read as children in his study."

"So they are likely to be out of my reach," Lord Pardes said.

"They are out of everyone's reach unless you are willing to ask him for them," Hertha replied.

"I do not think I am ready to do that," Lord Pardes said, "But I am sure I can find other books to read right here in the library. There are lots of interesting books in here, even if I had originally only wanted to read what was on my list. With the speed the trade agreement going it looks like I am going to have plenty of time to get some reading done. There were a few other books that looked interesting."

"There are plenty of interesting books in here," Hertha said, "If you get tired of non-fiction, there is plenty of good fiction."

"True," Lord Pardes said, "But you said the Hadden Grimes book you're your favourite story was gone."

"I can tell you the story," Hertha said.

"I would greatly appreciate hearing the story," Lord Pardes said, "If you do not mind and have the time."

"Those are not a problem," Hertha said, "The Prince and the Miller's daughters. Once upon a time…"

There was a small village near a river with a mill. The miller and his wife had three daughters. They were very proud of the oldest two daughters and were determined to help the girls improve their positions in life. The oldest daughter was given the best education the miller and his wife could afford. The daughter absorbed the knowledge presented to her and her teachers swore she was the smartest student they had ever taught. She learned everything they could teach her in a very short amount of time.

The middle daughter was beautiful, so they did what they could to make her even more beautiful. They found people who knew tricks that made the girl better looking than before. She was compared to many other girls and always declared more beautiful.

So, the miller and his wife put out the word they had daughters who were worthy of consideration by kings or princes. Then they sat back and waited. Several noblemen showed up, but all were turned away because none were good enough for the miller and his wife. Men from all over came to see the middle daughter and talk with the older daughter, but all the men were not deemed worthy to marry either daughter by the miller and his wife.

One day an unmarried prince and his entourage

arrived in a nearby town. They were there on their way from dealing with a hostile neighbouring kingdom and heading back to the capital city. They spent the night in the town, where they heard about these daughters of the miller who were beautiful and smart. At the urging on his men, the prince decided to visit the village and meet the miller's daughters. He sent a messenger before going saying he would arrive the next day.

The next day the prince and his entourage arrived as promised. The miller and his wife came out to greet them and welcome them to their home. The prince and his entourage left their horses for the youngest daughter to put them away with the help of an orphan boy who worked at the mill for food. The prince and the rest of the guests were brought into the house where they were seated in a large room created specifically for the viewing of the daughters. The oldest daughter was brought in and stood in front of the semi-circle of the people.

The oldest daughter was modestly pretty, but not really beautiful. She spent all afternoon answering the toughest questions the group of people could come up with. The prince did not give the girl any questions, but instead listened to her answer other people's question. At one point in the afternoon, the youngest daughter brought a cup of water to each member of the group before leaving again. She did this alone and was quiet while she did so. She never got in the way and was efficient at her job.

Once the afternoon had passed, the oldest daughter was removed from the room and supper was brought in for the group. It was as close to a feast as the miller could afford. The miller himself brought in the meat, and his wife brought in some of the rest of the food, but most of it was brought in by the youngest daughter. She was also the one who stayed to refill the cups as necessary and make sure each person was provided with everything they needed. The prince continued to sit quietly and watch everyone else. Many members of his entourage acted as if they were dining in the palace and there were plenty of servants to wait on them. The youngest daughter said nothing, but worked so efficiently none could complain about her skills.

After supper was finished and the youngest daughter had taken the dishes away as well as refilled the cups, the middle daughter was brought before the prince and his group. Her beauty was as they had been told. No woman any of them had ever seen was close to her in beauty. She turned and showed that all of her was evenly beautiful. She stripped down as much as modesty allowed so the group could see her beauty was not just her face and clothes.

Finally night fell and everyone was tired, so the miller and his wife offered the prince and his entourage rooms for the night. The prince accepted a room for himself and his two guards, but sent everyone else into the village to find rooms. The youngest daughter made the room ready for the prince and his guards to sleep. The guards double checked the room and the youngest daughter made any changes they felt were necessary. When everything was ready, the prince was allowed into the room and the youngest daughter wished them all a good night before leaving. The guards settled into their beds for the night, but the prince found himself staring at the ceiling.

The guards started to snore as the prince remained

awake. Getting tired of just lying there, the prince sat up. The guards did not move as he got out of bed and went to the window. He opened the shutters, sat down on the ledge, and then looked out. It was quiet outside with stars above and the moon shining down. He leaned back and relaxed in the cool air.

A rattling came from below and the prince looked down. The youngest daughter was hauling a bucket of water. She took it out toward the garden and poured it out at the base of some bushes. She went back to the well and refilled the bucket. The youngest daughter took the bucket back inside the kitchen door. The prince leaned back again. A while later the youngest daughter came back out with another bucket and dumped it out in bushes down from the ones she had watered earlier. This time she did not refill the bucket, but instead left it by the well before going back inside. When she came out the second time she was carrying a basket. The prince noticed the clothes the youngest daughter was pulling from the basket were the ones her sisters had worn earlier in the day. She put them up on the line. Her own clothes were the same dirty ones she had worn all day.

The prince expected her to pick up the basket and go back inside. But instead she went toward the river. She stopped on the bank and dropped to her knees. She bowed her head and folded her hands in front of her. She stayed there in prayer for several minutes. Some yelling came from the house, but the youngest daughter did not move for another minute. Then she got up and went back into the house. The yelling stopped once she was inside. She did not come back out as the prince watched. He eventually got tired and found he was able to sleep. He closed the shutters and went to bed.

The next morning, the prince and his guards were invited to join the miller, his wife, and their daughters for breakfast. The youngest daughter served them all. The older girls treated the youngest girl as if she was a servant and not their sister. The miller and his wife ignored the girl unless they felt the need to tell her to do something.

After breakfast the rest of the prince's entourage showed up and they were ready to go, but first the miller and his wife met with the prince and his entourage. Everyone looked at the prince and waited for his answer. The prince looked over the room and made everyone wait while he gathered his thoughts. Finally he started speaking.

"Thank you for your hospitality," the prince said, "The food has been wonderful and the beds comfortable. We appreciate meeting you and your daughters. The words which reached us the day before yesterday were you had daughters worthy of marrying princes, which we came to see. You showed us many things, not all of which you meant us to see. And I have determined that I wish to ask one of your daughters to marry me as long as you are willing."

The miller was willing to let the prince ask whichever of his daughters that caught the prince's attention. So, he called in his daughters. The older two came at their father's call, but the youngest also came into the room. She came to fill the cups people still had with them. The older two girls looked like they had prepared themselves for becoming engaged to the prince, but the youngest girl was prepared to be ignored.

The prince ignored the older girls and took the youngest daughter's hands. He took the jug of water away and set it down on the floor. He got down on his knee and looked up into the pretty eyes in the dirty face. And he begged her to marry him. She hesitated as everyone stared at them, but she did not look around at anyone else. Finally she said yes. The prince smiled, got to his feet, and embraced her. She hugged him back. Then they left together and his entourage followed them out. Her family stood there in shock unable to figure out what had happened.

Hertha finished the story and there was quiet in the library. Lord Pardes was quiet from where he was sitting and staring into space. He slowly came back to the present.

"That is a very good story," Lord Pardes said, "I can understand why you like it."

"I miss the book," Hertha said.

"Which is your favourite story from the book currently in the library?" Lord Pardes asked.

"Probably the Musician of Riverton," Hertha answered, "It is a story about a man who plays a lute and travels around until he reached Riverton, where he thinks he finds a home until someone decides he needs to move on. But he does find happiness in the end."

"Most of the time the story ends with the hero having a happy ever after," Lord Pardes said.

"Sometimes there are ones that are not happy at the end," Hertha said, "But usually they get something for their troubles. I do not mind if the endings are not happy, as long as the story is good."

"Most people like the stories where the person in the

story to get a satisfactory ending," Lord Pardes said, "It makes them think it is possible to have that kind of ending in their lives."

"I fully understand," Hertha said, "Is there any problem with having a happy ending?"

"Personally I will stick with hoping everything in my life turns out well," Lord Pardes said, "A happy ending has already been taken away from me."

Hertha was quiet because she was not sure what exactly to say. She recently learned life did not guarantee happy endings, but she knew what happened to her was not possible to be what caused Lord Pardes' life to lose its happy ending. However, she was not sure it was appropriate to ask, even if he had brought it up.

Lord Pardes seemed to have lost himself in thought and his eyes were unfocused. Hertha thought it was the end of the conversation, but he did not seem to be finished speaking.

"I was in the capital for my nineteenth birthday," Lord Pardes said, "There was this large party I went to and I met Leni there. She was the most beautiful woman I had ever seen in my life. She was the second daughter of a merchant. The oldest daughter had been married off to some great noble and Leni was engaged to a gentleman of similar place in society. But I introduced myself to her at the party, though I am still not sure how I ever got the courage to do so, and she decided she had fallen in love at first sight. We were happy together. She actually was not as extroverted as I first thought and we found we had lots of things in common. She asked her engagement be broken. Her father was not happy about it until she explained she had fallen in love with someone else. After meeting me, her father was willing to break off the engagement and let me marry her. He could see the love, which was the main reason, but it helped that I was still nobility and thus a step up socially from where she was.

"We were married within the week and she came back to the family estate with me. My parents got ready to name me heir, but did not do so because they wanted to make sure there was a child before they did so. My brother was married six months later. So, we were very happy for that first year, but there was no child at the end of it. It did not bother us because we were happy together and both of us were busy with things. The second year was a little rougher, but we still stuck together through it all. She had two miscarriages and it had detrimental effects on her health. She took a three month trip to the capital to visit her family to try and get some of her health back. She was slightly healthier when she came back, but we missed each other.

"It was our third wedding anniversary when she announced she was three months pregnant and both she and the baby were healthy so far. She was much happier as the months went on and both continued to be healthy. I spent less time in the library studying and a lot more time with her. She was excited and I helped her set everything up for when the baby was born.

"She was eight months along when it became clear there was something wrong. None of the doctors, or midwives could figure out what was wrong, or what to do about it. We tried everything we could, but nothing worked. Leni got to the point where she was not able to get out of bed and things were getting worse from there.

"I was called away to deal with a problem on the estate. It took a couple days so I have left instructions for someone to send for me if there were any changes. The first night out a messenger arrived to say Leni had lost the baby and she herself was fighting for her life. I raced home, but arrived too late. She was already gone and there was nothing I could do but mourn. That was about a year ago when all this happened, which is why I have spent more time with books than people."

"I understand," Hertha said, "My sister disappeared and it has taken a while for my parents to recover from it."

"I heard about Princess Narda," Lord Pardes said, "How are you dealing it?"

"We each had our own lives," Hertha said, "But it is strange not to have her around. I also did not think she is dead, but got herself into enough trouble she cannot get away from it. So, I do not have strong feelings of mourning over her being missing, but I do have an understanding of how others feel and how debilitating it can be."

"There have been some who feel I have been hiding from my responsibilities," Lord Pardes said, "With my brother taking over being heir that talk has slowed down. But my parents were still happy when I went to the capital to volunteer for this visit because they believe it is me coming out to hiding and back to life."

"They do not know about the books in the library?" Hertha said.

"No, they do not," Lord Pardes said, "But they do not need to know. They had enough problems dealing with the loss and then with me going back into my books. I do not want to take away what they want to believe."

"Was your request to go and study at the great

library done after your loss?" Hertha asked.

"Leni knew about and encouraged me," Lord Pardes answered, "She was the reason I did not withdraw my request. She would want me to do whatever I need to get opportunity, so that is what I am going to do."

"It is good to have reasons to keep going in life," Hertha said, "Without those it is harder to keep living.

"So I am learning," Lord Pardes said, "But it is a hard lesson. I very much appreciate hearing the story and the conversation, but I should get back. Perhaps we can talk another time." Lord Pardes got to his feet.

"I enjoyed our talk," Hertha said. She watched Lord Pardes leave the library. Then Hertha waited a few more minutes before trying to get to her feet. There were several waves of nausea that tried to stop her, but she just moved a little slower to avoid bringing anything up. She put the Hadden Grimes book in its proper place before leaving the library.

Hertha went back to her room. The maid had delivered a tray, which now sat on the table. Beside the tray was a folded note. Hertha ignored the tray, because the smell from the food made her stomach churn. Instead she picked up the note and unfolded it. All that was on it was the symbol Darwin drew to let Hertha know he was going to be waiting for her in the market place. Hertha had offered to teach Darwin how to read and write, but he had turned her down. It might have increased his skill set to improve what jobs he could do, but he had not been interested. Hertha had not bothered to offer it again; she just accepted the symbol as a message from him.

Hertha got herself dressed in her market place clothes before the maid could come back. Then she snuck through the castle to the kitchen door. No one stopped her. She went across the court yard with the same amount of attention. Outside the wall of the court yard, Hertha found Darwin leaning against the wall waiting for her.

"I was not sure you were going to come," Darwin said as they headed toward the market.

"I just got the note," Hertha said, "So I came as soon as I could."

"Sleeping late?" Darwin asked.

"I was having trouble sleeping, so I was in the library," Hertha answered, "Why did you want to go to the market place today?"

"The man with the meat is back," Darwin answered, "And I do not want miss out on the chance to have some more. I hope you did not eat too much for breakfast."

"I did not eat any breakfast," Hertha said, "I was not hungry at the time."

"Then you should have more room in your stomach for the delicious meat," Darwin said.

They reached the market place and headed down the street in search of the right smell. They caught it and followed it all the way to the meat vendor, who was happy to sell them each a piece carved off the large roast. Hertha expected her stomach to turn and everything to come back up. Instead the smell had her feeling hungry and the meat tasted delicious. The cider they found was the perfect to go with the meat, but Hertha turned down what Darwin had found them for dessert because the smell brought back visions of leaning over the bucket from earlier in the morning. Darwin just shrugged and ate that piece as well. They finished wandering through the market without seeing anything else they wanted and then headed back.

"So, how is the watch on the guards from Grankle?" Hertha asked.

"We are still going," Darwin answered, "But they have not actually been caught doing anything we can take back to Loic. And I think they know we are following them everywhere they go."

"Why?" Hertha asked.

"They are getting better at losing us and for longer intervals," Darwin answered, "Which is problematic and I think very troublesome. We do not know what they are up to, what they plan to do, how they planned to do it, what they have already know about the castle, and what they are doing in preparation. Unfortunately we cannot go through the suite and check it for anything. Nor can we make them stay where we can keep an eye on them. It is frustrating, but there is not much any of us can do about it without over stepping what we can do without repercussions for us."

"I saw one of the guards a few days ago," Hertha said, "He was in the market place and he was looking for someone or something. When he could not find it he went back to where he could see the side gate to the court yard and waited. I did not see what he was waiting for because I had to get in before it arrived. I went in the other side gate to avoid him seeing me."

"Probably a very good thing the guard did not see you," Darwin said, "Especially since we have no idea what their plan is yet."

"I would rather avoid them anyway," Hertha said.

"Probably a good idea," Darwin said.

"You should be careful too," Hertha said, "You do

not know what they will do if they catch you, even if they have not done anything yet."

"I will be," Darwin said.

They reached the court yard. Darwin went off in one direction and Hertha headed for the kitchen door. She reached it without any problem, but the kitchen was full. So Hertha had to sneak around the side, but once she was out of the kitchen and going through the hallways she did not have a problem.

The rest of the day was quietly spent in Hertha's room with a book she had been meaning to read. The only thing to disturb her was the maid retrieving the tray and bringing in another tray. Hertha found this food did not sit well when she tried a few bites, so she stopped before it brought up the meat from the market place. Eventually she fell asleep with the book in her hands and still dressed.

Hertha woke before day break and found herself sick again. She tried to go back to sleep, but her stomach would not let her. Finally she just lay there with the bucket under her head. It was a long time before she could sit up without leaning over the bucket. She sat there and finished reading the book. By the time she finished her stomach was doing better.

So, Hertha decided to take the book back to the library and put it back. She changed into some clean clothes before leaving her bedroom. Then she left her bedroom and headed to the library. The guard had fallen asleep at his post as he did not look up when she closed the door. His eyes were closed and there was a slight snore coming from him. Hertha did not bother with him because she preferred not have to answer any questions about what she was doing in the middle of the night.

The hallways were quiet as everyone else was still asleep. The castle steward was probably up and getting things ready for the day. The head cook was likely to be up and starting the bread for the day. But most of the rest of the castle was likely to be asleep, which meant she would not be bothered by anyone. She went into the library and found it as empty as she had hoped. Hertha lit the lamp and took it off the post to carry it with her.

It was easy to find the place the book belonged and thus she was able to put it back. There were other books she wanted, but she had left them in the library rather than take them to her room, so she started to look around for the one she wanted. She found three of the ones she wanted before she had to stop and sit down. The sun peeked over the horizon and lightened the sky. Hertha thought about getting up to take the books back to her room to avoid meeting anyone either here in the library or the hallway on the way back. But she could not move very far without the wave of nausea followed by her stomach contents welling up in her throat. She fought it, but it always caused her to lean back and rest.

When she had sat down, Hertha had picked a chair a few shelves off the main area. So she could see the light coming into the sky, but she was not visible to anyone coming in the door. So when the light from the window got bright enough, Hertha turned off the lamp to make herself even less visible to anyone coming in. But she was not entirely sure Lord Pardes would even show up in the library today because he had taken a new volume of the encyclopedia yesterday and it had taken him two days to read the last volume.

The sun came up and lit up the library. Hertha closed her eyes and let herself relax. It was warm in the library and the sun was comforting. With her eyes closed, Hertha felt like she was floating. It was like she was lying on a cloud with blue sky surrounding her. There was a slight breeze to keep from getting too warm. The cloud was soft and enveloping. It was warm enough that there was no need for a blanket.

The door of the library opened and closed, but it was so quiet and so far away, Hertha ignored it. There were footsteps with the person starting on the right side of the library while Hertha was sitting at the end of a shelf on the left side. Hertha did not hear the footsteps, or the person wandering around. The sky surrounded her and the rest of the world did not matter.

The library door creaked as it opened and then another creak as it closed. The footsteps on the right side of the room stopped and the person stood still. This new person did not quiet their footsteps, or avoid the squeaky spots. This person went straight down the main area of the library and straight to the window. This person did not sit down so it could not be Zebulon, because Zebulon would have sat down in the chair and started reading.

Hertha was still lost in her very relaxing place and did not let the footsteps, or presence, of the others in the room bother her. Her stomach did not bother her on her cloud. The waves of nausea had disappeared. All her other problems had faded away as well. There were no problems in this warm and comfortable place.

It was quiet in the library as Hertha sat in her chair, the one person at the window stood there and looked out, and the other person stood still without making a sound. The person at the window was the first to change positions. The person moved to the left side of the library. The footsteps started toward the first set of shelves. The person had just about to go between the shelves when they stopped and then started toward Hertha. She was slightly aware of them, but it did not disturb her.

"Are you okay?" it was Lord Pardes voice. Hertha was brought back to the chair she was sitting in, the sun in the room, and her problems had not gone away. She opened her eyes and looked up at Lord Pardes. He looked concerned about her.

"I am okay," Hertha said, "I was having trouble sleeping again and decided to come get some books. I just sat down for a minute."

"Perhaps you should head to bed and try again to get some sleep," Lord Pardes said, "Come on." Lord Pardes held out his hand. Hertha did not think about before taking his hand and let him help her get to her feet. The waves of nausea started, but Hertha swallowed them back as she picked up her books. Lord Pardes kept holding Hertha as they headed for the library door. He kept his pace slow enough she had no problem keeping up with him, but it was a very slow pace. They left the library behind and Hertha made sure they headed for her room. Hertha fought the whole way to keep her stomach contents down.

They reached it and found the guard was still asleep at his post. They moved around him and Lord Pardes opened the door for them. Inside everything was exactly as Hertha has left it. The maid had not shown up yet for the day. Lord Pardes guided Hertha to the bed where she sat down on it. Once she was sitting,

Hertha felt like she could not hold back any longer, but the bucket was right there in easy reach.

Lord Pardes took a step back and waited until she was finished. She laid back and closed her eyes. It was bad enough she could not keep anything down, but to be sick in front of Lord Pardes made everything worse. She felt his hand on her forehead and then he moved it to her cheek before removing it altogether. Hertha found that if she did not move her stomach did not either and so the contents stayed down.

There was the sound of a stool being dragged across the floor to be near the bed and then the creak as Lord Pardes sat down on it. He did not say anything at first as he sat there. Hertha kept her eyes closed, but she was not sleepy at the moment. She wanted to go back to the cloud she had been on, where all her problems were gone and she could relax. But it was impossible with Lord Pardes sitting in the room with her.

"Any other guard who slept like that would be asked to turn in his sword," Lord Pardes said, "I certainly would not accept that behaviour from my own guards, though I would be willing to take it from the guards the King of Grankle sent with me."

"No one had reported him," Hertha said, "And I did not mind. If he is awake he asks where I am going if it is not time for breakfast and he always thinks I am weird when I explain I am going to the library. If he is asleep it is convenient to me."

"But he is there to protect you," Lord Pardes said, "He cannot do it if he is asleep."

"There has not been any danger to me for a long time," Hertha said, "If there was some my father would tell me so that I would be watchful for it."

"Then why is there even a guard there?" Lord Pardes asked.

"Because occasionally Herwin or Garrick will talk Loic into putting guards on people's room as a precaution," Hertha answered, "He does it until the guards are needed for other things, or they leave him alone."

"If he wakes up before I leave he might be highly suspicious of what is going on in here," Lord Pardes said.

"My maid will be here before he wakes up," Hertha said, "She will understand somewhat if it is explained you found me in the library."

"Have you been this sick very long?" Lord Pardes asked.

"About a week," Hertha answered, "On and off. There are times when it is not as bad and times like this when it is worse."

"But no fever?" Lord Pardes asked, "That is slightly strange, usually when one is sick like that there is a fever to go with it."

"The sickness is not that kind," Hertha said, as she opened her eyes and looked at him. She did not want to outright tell him she was pregnant. She had not told anyone else and despite the friendliness between them over the past few days she was not sure it was a good idea to tell him the one thing she wanted to keep secret as long as possible. The three people who currently knew was likely three people too many, but the maid knew better than to spread things around and the housekeeper took her job too seriously to tell anyone else.

Lord Pardes was also too close to the cause of

Hertha's condition for her to want to tell him about the pregnancy. He might ask who the father was and Hertha might have to tell him it is Keften. And the Keften might be suggested to do the honourable thing, which was not anything Hertha wanted. She wanted to leave Keften out of the whole thing.

"I see," Lord Pardes said with a nod. It looked like one of those nods where he was trying for wise, but he had not worked out everything his mind had gathered to have a proper answer to what was going on.

"What were you doing in the library?" Hertha asked.

"Taking a break from reading," Lord Pardes answered, "I know it does not sound like the place to do that, but I have always been more comfortable in libraries than any other room. Also I do not know the castle well enough to have any idea where else I could go. And likely it is better to stay away from places people may find suspicious for me to go. I want to keep enough trust until the trade agreement has either been ratified, or nullified."

"The library has a good view of the court yard," Hertha said, "And the rising sun. I can understand going there to take a break." Hertha closed her eyes again.

"Where do you go to relax, besides the library?" Lord Pardes asked.

"Lately I have gone out to the garden," Hertha said, "It is beautiful out there with all the flowers blooming."

"There is a garden?" Lord Pardes asked, "I did not think there was room for a garden in the castle. The court yard is so large and the castle is right against the wall of the city."

"There is a garden," Hertha replied, "It is about the

same level as the court yard, but it is behind the throne room. It seems to have been built for the people living within the castle only. There is a lot more to the castle than most people see, or realize is there. There are even some parts that are never used. But I do not tend to wander the castle, though I did as a child. So, if I need some place to relax it is either here or the library with the garden being only occasionally."

"Where does your brother, Zebulon, disappear to for those couple hours in the afternoon?" Lord Pardes asked.

"The tower," Hertha answered.

"What does he do up there?" Lord Pardes asked.

"Look over the city, I think," Hertha answered, "He has been doing it every day for the last few months, but he did not do it as much before then. I think he found someone of interest in the city but has not gotten the nerve up to talk to her, I just do not know that for sure."

"So, there is nothing up in the tower?" Lord Pardes asked, "I would have thought there was a room up there or something."

"I do not know if there is or not," Hertha said, "I never venture up there. My father declared it an area not safe for us to go and so I never went up there. If there is a room up there, I do not think Zebulon goes into it."

"This whole castle is bigger than the one the King of Grankle lives in at the capital city," Lord Pardes said, "That one is about half the size of this one. As we were riding up through the streets of the city to this one I wondered how people avoided getting lost, but once inside I noticed it was not too bad as far as figuring out where everything was. I also have not gone too far out of the areas I know. So, I know where my suite is, the library, the throne room, and your father's study, but not much else. And likely I will never need to find anything else because the trade agreement will be dealt with before then."

The door opened the maid came in carrying a tray of food. She looked at Hertha lying on the bed and Lord Pardes sitting on the stool near the bed. She did not say anything and her expression did not change as she put the tray on the table and left the room.

"Apparently not curious," Lord Pardes said as he got to his feet. He went over to the tray and poured a cup of water before coming back to the bed. He offered Hertha the cup. She took it and sat up enough to drink from it. Lord Pardes stood there until she was finished and handed the cup back to him. He took it back to the tray before sitting back down on the stool.

"Thank you," Hertha said.

"You are welcome," Lord Pardes said, "Feeling a little better?"

"A little bit," Hertha said, "But it usually gets better about this time, so I can do other things. With the exception of eating that is."

"At least there is some time when you can do things during the day," Lord Pardes said, "But the symptoms seem more like what Leni called morning sickness than an actual illness. Hers were severe bouts of it and it never just showed up in the morning, so I'm not sure why she called it morning sickness. The doctor said it was normal for women who were pregnant to suffer from it. I did not believe him until my brother's wife also suffered from it during her pregnancy. But she only suffered from it for a few months and Leni was still suffering from it right up to the eighth month."

"I have only had this for a week," Hertha said, "I do not know how long it will last."

"Are you actually pregnant?" Lord Pardes asked.

"The housekeeper seemed to think so the first morning I was sick," Hertha said, "But the only thing I have been dealing with is the being sick."

"The lack of other symptoms suggest to me you are pregnant," Lord Pardes said, "From my understanding it is the number of symptoms over a period of time that makes most women figure it out what is going on, though a few know it right away. The biggest question there is whether you have a lover and whether when you pay attention to your body enough to know whether you find there are other changes you have not noticed suggesting you are pregnant."

"I have thought about it," Hertha said, "I am pregnant, but I have not told anyone yet."

"I will not tell anyone," Lord Pardes said, "It is your news to share and not mine in any way."

"Thank you," Hertha said, "I really appreciate it."

"However, I do warn you people will notice given enough time," Lord Pardes said.

"I know," Hertha said, "I just am not ready to deal with it all."

"There is that," Lord Pardes said, "It can be a stressful time to tell people about something like that. Is the father going to be there for you?"

"No," Hertha said, "He does not know and I will not be telling him. He does not know I am sick because I have not met with him since I found out myself."

"Sounds like you are cutting him off without finding out if he has any interest in being a father," Lord Pardes said.

"I am not going to marry him," Hertha said, "It was not that kind of relationship and as far as I am concerned it is over."

"That does not sound like it was a good ending," Lord Pardes said.

"I am not sure he noticed I have not gone in search of him, or sent him a message in a while," Hertha said, "It certainly did not look like it when I saw him the one day in the garden. But I knew what kind of relationship it was the whole time it was going on."

"That does not stop the sting when you see the person with someone else," Lord Pardes said, "It is just something more to tell yourself to avoid feeling upset over the whole thing. It really does not mean much as far as getting over the person, especially if you are carrying their child."

"You think I should tell him," Hertha said.

"I think he should probably be given a chance to know his child," Lord Pardes said, "But I am speaking as a man who never got the chance to meet any of my children and had been looking forward to holding each of them. And what will your parents think and say when they find out you are pregnant? Many times there is a demand of marriage between you and the father."

"My parents will not make such a demand," Hertha said, "They will suggest a marriage would be a good idea, but they will not demand it is the child's father. The marriage will be just to save them from embarrassment of having their daughter unmarried with a child. Or I could avoid it all and find some way to disappear into the country with the child so no one ever knows about it all."

"But you really have not figured out what to do," Lord Pardes said.

"No, I have not figured out what to do," Hertha said, "But I will before I have to start telling people."

"I do not mean to pry, and I know it is none of my business," Lord Pardes said, "But who is the father?"

Hertha was silent for a few minutes as she contemplated tell him. He waited for her to say something. She still was not sure about saying anything, but there was something somewhere telling her it was okay.

"Keften," Hertha finally said.

"As in my assistant Keften?" Lord Pardes asked.

"Yes," Hertha answered.

"I had been wondering what he was doing with his time," Lord Pardes said, "But I did not think he would be doing that."

"Why not?" Hertha asked.

"He had been known for finding ladies to spend time with," Lord Pardes said, "But I thought he had stopped when he had gotten married four years ago. He and his wife have two children and another on the way."

Hertha nodded, but she did not cry, scream, display anger, or change expression in any way.

"You suspected something like that?" Lord Pardes asked.

"Not exactly," Hertha answered, "I just spent some time thinking about it after I saw him with the serving girl and figured I was not his only lover. With that comes the thoughts of why waste time and energy on him."

"That is a good way to think about things," Lord Pardes said, "Did you want something to eat or drink?"

"Drink, maybe," Hertha answered, "But I do not want anything to eat."

Lord Pardes got up and went over to the tray. He picked up one of the chunks of bread and smeared butter on it before picking up the cup and going back to the bed. He handed Hertha the cup before taking a bite of the bread.

"They send you up different stuff than they send me," Lord Pardes said as sat back down on the stool.

"They do not care if you get fed, or if you enjoy it," Hertha said, "I am closer to being important around here. And the housekeeper probably has left instructions with the head cook about what I am to get and not get."

"Tastes better than what I get too," Lord Pardes said.

"Go ahead and eat it," Hertha said, "I will not be."

"Thank you," Lord Pardes said. He left her to sip from the cup and sat down at the tray. He started to eat. Hertha did not move unless it was to take another sip from the cup. When the cup was empty she set it on the floor and closed her eyes once again. It was not long before she had fallen asleep.

Lord Pardes finished eating before getting up. He went over to the bed and checked on her. Hertha was fast asleep. He picked up the cup and took it back to the tray. Then he left the room. The guard was not there when Lord Pardes stepped into the hallway, neither was anyone else. He headed to his own suite for the day.

Hertha slept the rest of the day and well into the night without being disturbed. When she did wake up it was because of the waves of nausea were back and though she did not bring anything up, Hertha spent the rest of the night lying so her head was over the bucket.

The maid had already brought in the tray and brought over the cup as Hertha request before leaving, when there came a knock at the door.

"Come in," Hertha called. The door opened and Lord Pardes stepped inside. He came over to the stool and sat down.

"How are you doing?" Lord Pardes asked.

"About the same as yesterday," Hertha answered, "But I was thinking of seeing if I could find something to eat that would stay down. How about yourself?"

"I am fine," Lord Pardes said, "But I have been thinking."

"About what?" Hertha asked.

"About your problems as well as my own," Lord Pardes said, "There may be a solution to both."

"What is that?" Hertha asked.

"A marriage between us," Lord Pardes said, "It would mean you would be married before everyone finds out you are pregnant. We would be gone from court shortly so people would not be able to tell how soon after the wedding the child was born. The child would never be an heir to any estate, but would be well cared for. You would never be wanting, except for entertainment if I do get accepted to study at the great library. The pressure for me to find someone else would disappear. But there would be no expectations of a usual marriage unless you choose there to be. I guarantee Keften will not be around. I had decided even before this idea came to me he needed a job somewhere else with his wife and children close by to watch over him."

Lord Pardes paused and looked at Hertha. She was

quiet and appeared to be thinking about it. There was a slight look of relief on his face because she had not outright refused, but there was a look of uncertainty as well. He left her to think about for several minutes and picked up one of the books from beside the bed. He flipped through the pages and read a little here and there before putting it back. He did this with two more before Hertha looked up at him.

"What do you think?" Lord Pardes asked, "Will you marry me?"

"On those terms, I will marry you," Hertha said, "But you will have to get permission from my father and he will be harder to persuade."

"I will make an appointment with him as soon as possible to ask his permission," Lord Pardes said, "I just wanted to make sure you agreed before going to him."

"You can now go to him, ..." Hertha paused at the end as if grasping for a name and not wanting to call him Lord Pardes.

"Seath," Lord Pardes supplied.

"Seath," Hertha finished.

"I will go see if I can make the appointment," Lord Pardes said, "You see if you can find something you can eat."

"I will," Hertha said. Lord Pardes got up and left Hertha's room. Hertha laid there for several more minutes before ringing the bell beside her bed. The maid appeared within a minute.

"My stomach does not agree with anything on this tray," Hertha said when the maid was close enough, "Go ask the cook what else is ready and bring me back the answer so I can find something my stomach is willing to keep down."

"Right away," the maid curtsied and then left the room. Hertha took another sip from the cup and let her mind go over what just happened.

LORD PARDES ASKS FOR HERTHA'S HAND AND PROSTER MUST MAKE SOME DECISIONS

Proster was sitting at his desk working on paperwork as he tried to exercise his left hand as Dr. Kayson told him to. His hand was doing better after the last attack than the first one, but it was still a lot of work. There came a knock on the door. Proster did not remember scheduling any meetings and there was nothing on the piece of paper which he had started writing things down on.

"Come in," Proster called. The door opened and the steward stepped inside.

"I am sorry to disturb you," the steward said, "But Lord Pardes would like to make an appointment to talk to you."

"The meeting to talk about the trade agreement was yesterday," Proster said, "So, he cannot be interested in talking about it, unless he wants to drop it altogether because it is taking too long."

"He did not tell me why, only that he wished you would agree to see him," the steward said.

Proster looked at the sheet of paper with his schedule. After a moment he looked up at the steward.

"I can see him tomorrow afternoon," Proster said, "It is the only time I have available until next week."

"I will let you know if he prefers next week," the steward said, "Otherwise I will not disturb you again."

"I accept that," Proster said. The steward slipped out of the room and closed the door behind him. Proster went back to his paperwork.

The next afternoon there was a knock on Proster's study door. He had taken a break from work of any kind and was reading. He looked up from his book and checked his schedule. It told him he had an appointment with Lord Pardes today, which did not make sense. They had talked about the trade agreement only a couple days ago and there was nothing to say about it unless Lord Pardes was pulling out and leaving. Since Proster was not sure what Lord Pardes' agenda was it did not make sense for him to be leaving yet. For one thing the guards were still wandering the hallways as if searching for something and Lord Pardes was not likely to leave until he found it. But what else could Lord Pardes possibly want?

The knocking came again. Proster stuck a paper into the book to make his spot and then slid the book back on the shelf. Then he made sure he was presentable and his left hand was sitting on his knee.

"Come in," Proster called. The door opened and

Lord Pardes stepped inside. He closed the door behind him before bowing to Proster. Lord Pardes was without his assistant today and he was dressed a little more causal, but still fit to visit a king.

"Rise," Proster said, "And explain yourself." Lord Pardes straightened up and looked at Proster. He seemed extra nervous today, but he held it in check very well.

"It is a personal matter I wish to discuss with you today," Lord Pardes said.

"If you wish to use big words, grand gestures, and long winded explanation, we are in the wrong room," Proster said impatiently.

"I wish to ask for your daughter, Hertha's, hand in marriage," Lord Pardes said.

"Does it not feel better to get rid of all the pretenses?" Proster asked, "It just makes everything less complicated."

"Yes, sire," Lord Pardes answered. His nervousness had gone up a little bit.

"What does Hertha say to this proposition?" Proster asked.

"She is agreeable to it," Lord Pardes answered.

"Do you love her?" Proster asked.

"I have learned to," Lord Pardes answered, "And I expect to learn to love her even more."

"You are aware I have lost one daughter fairly recently?" Proster asked.

"I know," Lord Pardes answered.

"You are also aware there is no place in this kingdom for you, even if there is plenty of room for her?" Proster asked.

"Yes," Lord Pardes answered, "There is very little

room for me at home, but if God smiles down on me I will be granted my request to study at the great library. To be there is to in neither the Kingdom of Proster nor Grankle."

"Well thought out," Proster said, "I will think about your request and let you know my answer within two days."

"Very well," Lord Pardes said with a bowed, "I await your judgement."

"Dismissed," Proster said. Lord Pardes bowed again before leaving the study and closing the door behind him. Proster wrote out notes on everything that had just happened to make sure he did not forget any part of it. He was going to have to think about all of it for a while and needed all the information to make the decision.

Proster put down his pen when he was finished and stared at the paper. The last thing in the world he expected when Lord Pardes knocked on the door would be a request for marriage to Hertha. Proster did not remember any connection between Lord Pardes and Hertha being mentioned or seen in the time Lord Pardes had been in the Kingdom of Proster. And they definitely had not met before then.

Proster remembered the Pardes family. They were one of those who did not spend any time at the capital and usually stayed out of politics unless they had no other choice. They had been supporters of Proster's men when they fought for Grankle. They also paid their share when they needed the protection, but they were not going to go up against the king and his belief in not paying the army.

Lord Pardes did not admitted to being in love or that Hertha was in love with him. Proster studied those notes on the paper. The young man had evaded the question as if it mattered less than the fact they had agreed to get married. Proster had not spent any time with Hertha lately, which he knew was a mistake, so he did not know what was going on in her life. However, could she really be willing to marry Lord Pardes on the thought she would learn to love him, but not currently be in love with him? There was something wrong there in Proster's mind. It did not seem quite like his daughter. Proster wrote a note below the ones on his conversation with Lord Pardes to go and talk with Hertha as soon as he had some time.

Hertha sat cross legged on her bed with the meal tray in front of her when there was a knock at the door. The maid got up from the stool and went to answer it. She opened it enough to see who it was before opening it the rest of the way and letting the person in. Seath stepped into the room.

"You are dismissed," Hertha said meeting the maid's eyes.

"Yes, Miss," the maid curtsied before leaving. She closed the door behind her. Seath sat down in the chair which had been moved to the place where the stool had been.

"How are you feeling?" Seath asked.

"I can eat a little bit today," Hertha answered, "But I do not want to eat too much because it is likely to come back later. What happened?"

"I just talked to your father," Seath answered, "Today was the only time he had available to meet until next week."

"What did he say?" Hertha asked.

"He would think about it," Seath answered, "I think he hesitates because I did not say we were in love."

"He would be concerned about that," Hertha said, "But it does not mean he will say no. When did he say he would give you an answer?"

"He did not specify," Seath answered, "I expect he will send for me when he has his answer."

Hertha nodded but did not say anything.

"I told him about my waiting for word on whether I got to study at the Great Library," Seath said, "Hopefully it helps him with the decision. The trade agreement I was sent to negotiate is now dead, so once your father gives me his decision I have to start making preparations to head home."

"I am sorry if you did not get all your reading done," Hertha said.

"The only books I did not get to read were the ones I could not find in the library," Seath said, "I have done what I set out to do, it was just a matter of how long the treaty negotiations would drag out before someone shut it down. I did not think it was going to go anywhere anyway."

"The King of Grankle will be disappointed in you," Hertha said.

"He can say whatever he wants when he receives my report," Seath said, "I figured on going straight to the family estate and skipping the trip to the capital. Since I would not be the first to do such a thing, I doubt there will be repercussions."

"Okay," Hertha said, "Hopefully, my father will reach his decision soon."

"I hope so as well," Seath said.

After supper, Proster headed up to Hertha's room. She had not been at supper and he could not remember seeing her for several days. But with his memory he could have run into her yesterday and not know it. The guard was not at his post. Proster checked his temper as he had never specifically said day and night. Though why the guard would not realize he would not have meant it was beyond Proster. He would have to send the different instructions to the guard.

Proster knocked on the door. The door opened a moment later and the maid, after seeing who it was, opened it all the way before going down in a curtsy. Proster thought about telling her to skip it, but he instead just stepped into the room. Hertha was sitting on the couch with a book in her hands. She had looked up from it to see who was at the door.

"Good evening," Proster said.

"Good evening," Hertha said, "Come in and have a seat."

Proster did so as Hertha waved to the maid that she was dismissed. The maid left the room and shut the door.

"I had Lord Pardes visit me this afternoon," Proster said once Hertha had found a bookmarker and set the book down on the table.

"He said he was going make an appointment to see you," Hertha said.

"Then you know his request?" Proster asked.

"Yes," Hertha answered, "He asked me first before going to you so he was not being presumptuous."

"Do you love him?" Proster asked.

"I am learning to," Hertha answered. Proster could see the truth in the statement and sensed there was much more to this than love, but also there seemed to be a resolution. She would go through with it because the marriage got her something she felt she needed and she would love Lord Pardes over time. It disappointed Proster a little to see his child settling for something less than true love, but he had also been around too long to think everyone found their true love immediately. Sometimes it took many years of living with 'settled for what was there' to realize the person was the true love and it just had not been visible until then.

"You know his guards have been wandering the castle at night and going places they should not with a plan no one knows anything about, except maybe Lord Pardes?" Proster asked.

"Yes," Hertha answered, "But I do not think he wishes the kingdom any harm, even if the guards do."

"Unfortunately, what the guards do rests on his head as leader of the delegation," Proster said.

"So, what is your answer?" Hertha asked.

"I will think about it and give my answer within two days," Proster said.

"I see," Hertha said.

Proster got up and went over to his daughter. He hugged her close.

"It will turn out as it is meant to be," Proster said, "It always does." She nodded, but did not say anything. Proster finally let go.

"Good night," Proster said.

"Good night," Hertha said.

Proster left Hertha's room and went up to his own. The guard at his door nodded to him as Proster entered. Proster nodded back. Inside Ruana was seated on her chair working on her needle work piece. She looked up at Proster and smile. Proster smiled back before sitting down on the couch. She went back to her needle work and he sat in silence.

"What is it?" Ruana finally broke the silence.

"My world is changing faster than I know how to keep up with," Proster answered. Ruana set her needle work to one side and turned to face Proster.

"What happened?" Ruana asked.

"I need to start at the beginning and tell you things I should have told you before," Proster said.

Ruana was quiet as she waited for him to start.

"About a month ago I collapsed in the throne room," Proster said, "The guard sent for a doctor, who told me a large part of it was stress and it might be possible for my body to recover. However, I had a second attack and he has since determined my body is unlikely to recover and as long as I follow his recommendations I keep myself alive longer."

Ruana sat without moving and her eyes on her clasped hands. She did not say anything and Proster let her digest the news. Finally she looked up at him with tears in her eyes.

"How long?" Ruana asked.

"Six months to a year," Proster answered, "I am hoping for the year, but it may not happen. Over that time period my condition is going to deteriorate and things are going to get worse for me."

"Is there anything I can do?" Ruana asked.

"There is nothing anyone else can do about it," Proster said, "But I would rather you went back to your family's estate during the time. I am hiding what I can from people, but I do not want to hide it from you. I would rather you were not here to watch me die."

Ruana was silent for several minutes. He could tell she wanted to stay, but she also wanted to honour his request.

"What about Zebulon and Hertha?" Ruana asked.

"Zebulon needs to be taught how to rule the kingdom since it is going to become his," Proster said, "That is why I am hoping for the year, so I can teach him what he needs to know. He does not need to know all of this, only that he is loved and needs to take care of the kingdom. Hertha is the other reason I needed to talk to you. Lord Pardes has asked for her hand in marriage."

"He is the nobleman from Grankle, is he not?" Ruana asked.

"He is," Proster answered, "Apparently they met and have reached the decision to marry each other."

"You do not believe they love each other?" Ruana asked.

"They may, one day," Proster said, "But today is not that one day."

"It is better than many people get," Ruana said, "And if they reached the agreement then they must have a reason even if they are not willing to share it."

"You think I should let them get married?" Proster asked.

"Marriage is not something to take lightly," Ruana said, "And if they have decided to take that step then they have a good reason."

Proster nodded but did not say anything.

"Once they are married and headed back to Grankle, I will head out to my family estate," Ruana said.

"Then I'll let them know my decision in the morning," Proster said.

Ruana reached over and took Proster's hand. She squeezed it and he squeezed back. They sat there for several minutes without speaking.

"I love you," Proster said.

"I know," Ruana said, "And I love you too."

"I am scared of what is happening to me," Proster said, "And what it means for my kingdom."

"Zebulon will be a good king once you have taught him what you can," Ruana said.

"If I can get him to put the books down long enough to see the real world," Proster said, "At the moment, my biggest fear with him is that he will be easily manipulated by those who would choose to destroy everything I have built."

"Then you need to start your lessons there," Ruana said.

"He also needs to get the courage up to talk to the woman," Proster said, "And quit watching her from a distance."

"He will," Ruana said, "He just needs a little time. Our children need to learn things on their own. Zebulon will find his place as king, Hertha will discover love, and Narda will make you proud."

"And you?" Proster asked.

"I will miss the other half of my soul for the length of time we are separated," Ruana said, "I would rather be here where you are and support you through everything, but I will do what you ask because you ask it of me. I hope you find the peace you need."

"Thank you," Proster said before taking his wife into his arms. They held on to each other.

Proster went down to his study when Ruana went

back to her needle work. It was a quiet evening and he needed to get attend to some issues.

Proster sat in his study reading through the various papers that had been left on his desk as if he would actually get to them. Nothing looked urgent so he had not done any of the work involved with any of them. It was far enough past his bedtime he expected to end up sleeping in tomorrow to catch up, so he did not want to get too involved in anything that would keep him up later. He was getting close to the bottom of the stack and was looking forward to heading upstairs to bed when there came a pounding at his study door. It was getting to be too late for the steward to be up and everyone else was surely already asleep. The pounding did not stop.

"Come in," Proster called. The pounding stopped as the door opened and Darwin stood in the doorway. The young man was out of breath and worried.

"What is it?" Proster said.

"The guards from Grankle have kidnapped Hertha," Darwin said, "They have her near the back door."

Proster got to his feet and grabbed his sword as he followed Darwin out of the study. Darwin took the lead as they hurried up to the back door. Darwin had not caught his breath yet and Proster found himself breathing hard after the first set of stairs. They were just passed area where Zebulon and Hertha's rooms were when they came across Lord Pardes in the hallway.

"What is going on?" Lord Pardes asked seeing them rushing passed.

"Your guards have taken Hertha hostage," Proster said, "And we need to get to the back door before they do anything else foolish."

"They are not my guards specifically," Lord Pardes said as he joined them, "They were sent with me by the King of Grankle. I did not want them along, but I did not have a choice."

"Well, you needed to keep a better eye on them," Darwin said, "They have been wandering around without escort planning whatever they are doing now since you got here."

"I apologize for that," Lord Pardes said, "I did not think they were doing anything so troubling."

"We can sort it out later," Proster said as they continued on.

They went up the next series of stairs and finally reached the hallway where the back door was. The two guards were there, one working on the lock on the door while the other stood back and watched. Hertha and Ruana were unconscious and tied together near the door with another coil of rope lying nearby. Both guards heard the three coming and looked up.

They stood up and drew their weapons. Proster brought his up, and Darwin pulled out a knife, and Lord Pardes took out a dagger he had with him.

"What do you think you are doing?" Lord Pardes demanded.

"What we were ordered to do," the one guard said, "Our king gave us orders and we will complete them no matter what. Your mission is a waste of time, but it gave us plenty of time to do what needed to be done. Now nothing will stop us."

"We are here and we are going to stop you," Proster said as he started toward the guards.

"I hardly think so," the guard replied, "You forgot to call your army to help you."

"I do not need my army for the two of you," Proster said.

Proster reached them and started his attack. The guard countered. Darwin and Lord Pardes took on the other guard. Every time Proster attacked the guard countered, but the guard never had enough time to make his own attack. They continued with Proster attacking and the guard countering. If Proster had been in better shape the fight would have been over very quickly, but his weakened state made the fight stretch out. Proster felt himself tiring, but he refused to let it show or affect his swing. He attacked the guard and the guard countered, but was driven back into the wall. The guard tried to push back. Proster would not let himself be pushed. Proster attacked and the guard rolled to the left to avoid being hit. Proster had turned and was attacking again when the guard managed to straighten up. He barely blocked the swing.

Darwin and Lord Pardes were trying to stay out of the reach of the guard's sword while still within range of their blades. There was ducking and weaving, but neither side could get a hit. The guard kept swinging at them and they kept evading the swings. The guard was able to keep both of them on one side of him, so with each swing he had a high possibility of hitting one of them. Darwin would try to duck in and jab the guard with his knife. If the sword swing did not keep Darwin away, the guard would use his foot. Lord Pardes had a harder time getting close to the guard as he was not able to duck like Darwin could. Instead he worked to distract the guard while Darwin tried to get close with his knife.

The guard, who was fighting Proster, was out of breath and missed blocking one of Proster's swings.

Proster's sword ripped through the cloth of his shirt neck above the armour because the guard had managed to stagger back enough the sword did not reach the skin. Proster was quick to attack again and the guard blocked it. The guard tried to break free and attack, but found before he could attack he was blocking Proster's attack. Proster pushed the guard backward until he was again backed into the wall.

Darwin jabbed at the guard again, but the guard kicked the knife forcing Darwin back out of range. Lord Pardes moved toward the guard to distract and give Darwin time to recovered, but the guard swung his sword at both of them. Darwin and Lord Pardes dodged back out of the way. The guard followed and swung again. Darwin got out of the way in time, but the sword went across Lord Pardes' front and ripped his shirt. Lord Pardes went farther backward to get away from the sword. Darwin ducked under the next swing and tried to get close with his knife again. The guard kicked at Darwin, this time hitting him in the chest. Darwin fell on his back. The guard was about to take advantage of that when Lord Pardes threw his dagger at the guard, which went passed his head close enough to scratch his cheek. The guard turned from Darwin long enough to swing his sword at Lord Pardes, who had to jump back. Darwin brought his knife up to stab it though the guard's leg. Before he could, the guard noticed and kicked his arm. The knife went skittering across the floor until it bumped into the wall. Darwin rolled away from the guard and his sword in the direction of the knife. The guard ignored him in favour of swing at Lord Pardes again as Lord Pardes tried to get closer to him.

Proster swung and the guard blocked it. Proster felt the strength was draining from his left arm and knew he had to finish this fight as quickly as he could. He attacked again, but this time when the guard blocked it, Proster brought his elbow up and connected with the guard's nose. The guard ducked down, but there was a trickle of blood coming from his nose. He ignored it as he blocked Proster's swing. Proster followed the swing with a high knee to the guard's stomach. The guard felt the air leave him and gasped for some as he collapsed to the floor. Proster swung at him again. The guard rolled out of range, but did not avoid Proster's foot which connected with his lower back.

Darwin grabbed his knife and got back into the fight just in time to distract the guard from putting his sword through Lord Pardes' gut. Instead Lord Pardes got another rip in his shirt. The guard swung at Darwin and Lord Pardes to keep them at a distance. Both backed off a step, but quickly moved forward once the swing was over. Darwin ducked under the start of the next swing and Lord Pardes to one side. The guard kicked Darwin over again and thrust toward Lord Pardes. The sword went through the side of Lord Pardes shirt and cut his side enough for blood to show, but not enough to slow him down. He moved in closer as the guard tried to kick Darwin's knife away again.

Proster finally hit the guard on the side of his head with the flat of the sword. There was enough force behind the blow the guard collapsed into a heap on the floor. Proster turned to the other fight. They were still going at it. Then Lord Pardes accidently stepped on the guard's foot. This of course caused the guard to shout in pain as he barely missed Darwin with his sword.

Proster used the distraction to stick his leg out and cause the guard to trip. The guard fell flat on his face. Darwin used the opportunity to sit on the guard's back while Lord Pardes took away the guard's sword. Proster grabbed the rope and started to tie the guard up. Once he was secured, Proster tied up the other one.

Lord Pardes and Darwin got busy cutting Hertha and Ruana free. The ladies were still unconscious. Footsteps came down the hallway causing the three of them to look up. It was Thane and Loic coming toward them.

"Those two need to be taken to the dungeon," Proster ordered pointing to the two guards.

"Yes, Sire," Loic said. He and Thane each took one of the guards and dragged them off. Lord Pardes picked up Hertha and headed down the hallway. Darwin was just about to go after them when he noticed Proster was struggling to keep his own feet. Darwin picked up Ruana and led the way down the hallway. They went to Proster and Ruana's bedroom. Darwin laid Ruana down on the bed while Proster sat down on the couch.

"Have Thane send for Dr. Kayson," Proster said.

"Yes, Your Majesty," Darwin said before leaving the room.

Darwin found Thane and Loic coming out of the door to the dungeon. They looked up at him as he came down the hallway toward them.

"How are Ruana and Hertha?" Loic asked.

"They are still unconscious," Darwin answered, "King Proster asked for Thane to send for Dr. Kayson."

"Who is Dr. Kayson?" Loic asked turning to Thane.

"The doctor who has been treating King Proster," Thane answered.

"Go get him," Loic said, "He can probably make sure Ruana and Hertha are all right while he is here."

"Yes, sir," Thane said and then hurried off.

"I should have you and your friends beaten," Loic turned to Darwin, "If you knew about those two sneaking around you should have reported, not taken it upon yourselves to follow them. You put the people of this kingdom in danger."

"When Riller tried to tell you about it, you dismissed him without listening to him because he was the stable master's son and not one of your guards," Darwin said, "We were trying to find evidence we could bring to you that would make you listen. If you have listened to begin with we would not had to do any of it and this would not have happened."

"And stealing armour out of our armoury was not enough for you to report them?" Loic demanded.

"We did not think it was enough," Darwin said, "Because it was only the once and they used it to check out the city. Anyone with any knowledge can find out there are no weaknesses in the city walls."

"Had you brought that evidence to me, I would have had guards to keep them in line," Loic said.

"King Proster knew about the guards wandering the castle," Darwin said.

"He is leaves worrying about the security of this castle to me," Loic said, "So the next time you find evidence people here are in danger, you bring it to me."

"Yes, sir," Darwin said.

Loic turned and stalked away. Darwin stood there until Loic was out of sight. Then he slipped into the shadow across from the door to the dungeon. He got comfortable as he figured he was going to end up standing guard all night.

Dr. Kayson followed Thane up the stairs of the castle. They arrived at the door to the room King Proster shared with his wife. The guard stepped aside. Thane knocked.

"Come in," Proster's voice called from inside. Thane opened the door and held it for Dr. Kayson. Once Dr. Kayson was inside, Thane closed the door. Proster was sitting in the chair. He looked pale, but otherwise okay. Ruana was lying on the bed. She had not regained consciousness.

"How are you feeling?" Dr. Kayson asked Proster as he went over to the bed.

"Tired," Proster answered.

"Anything else?" Dr. Kayson asked as he started his examination of Ruana.

"Not really," Proster answered, "I feel a little weak, but I remember so many fights where I sliced right through my opponents without difficulty. Compared to then I am weak now. How is Ruana?"

"She appears to have been knocked out with an herb extract," Dr. Kayson answered, "Aside from a few bruises, she is not injured. She should wake up in a few hours with no ill effects."

Dr. Kayson left Ruana and went over to where Proster was sitting.

"How is your left hand?" Dr. Kayson asked.

"It goes through times when it does not work properly," Proster answered, "But otherwise is getting stronger when I remember to exercise it."

"That is good," Dr. Kayson said, "Hopefully, things will continue as they have been."

Proster nodded.

"Rest for now," Dr. Kayson said before turning to Thane, "I believe you said there was someone else I should check on."

"Hertha was also knocked out," Thane said, "Her room is the floor below this one. I will show you the way."

"All right," Dr. Kayson said. Thane led the way out of the room. The guard stepped back in front of the door as soon as they were headed down the hallway.

Dr. Kayson followed Thane back to the stairs, where they went back down a floor and along the winding corridor until they reached another door with a guard standing in front of it. The guard stepped aside at Thane's nod. Thane opened the door for Dr. Kayson and then followed him inside.

Hertha was lying unconscious on the bed while Lord Pardes was sitting on a chair that had been moved to the side of the bed. Lord Pardes looked up at them.

"I am Dr. Kayson," Dr. Kayson said as he came over to Lord Pardes, "I was asked to come check on Hertha."

"I am Lord Pardes," Lord Pardes said standing to shake the offered hand and then he stepped back away from the bed. Dr. Kayson started his examination of Hertha as Lord Pardes joined Thane near the door.

"She was knocked out using the same herb extract as Ruana," Dr. Kayson said, "Also similar to Ruana, aside from some bruises she has not been injured. She should be fine when she wakes up in a few hours."

"Thank you," Lord Pardes said.

"Everything else is fine too," Dr. Kayson said looking at Lord Pardes, who nodded in response. Thane pretended to have no idea what they were talking about and no interest.

"Now, I suppose there ware guards who need medical attention," Dr. Kayson said going over to stand near Thane. Lord Pardes went back to sitting in the chair by the bed.

"This way," Thane said leading Dr. Kayson out of the room.

Dr. Kayson found the guards to be fine, except for some scratches, bruises, and bumps on the head, before leaving the castle for the night.

Loic had checked to make sure both guards at Hertha's door had the proper instructions to not let anyone in before heading to Proster and Ruana's room. He met up with Proster, who was going the other way, in the hallway.

"Should you not be resting?" Loic asked.

"I should be," Proster answered, "But my mind will not rest until I know what those two were planning to do. Lord Pardes did not know and did not support it. That suggests to me the whole plan is the idea of the King of Grankle." Proster went passed Loic and Loic had to turn to follow him.

"How can you be sure about Lord Pardes' role in the plan?" Loic asked.

"Because he helped to subdue them," Proster answered, "He also said he did not know about what the two men have been doing around the castle since their arrival. I believe him because this morning he asked for Hertha's hand in marriage."

"Okay," Loic said, "The men have been shackled along the dungeon wall."

"Good," Proster said, "I am going to have a long,

and possibly painful, talk with them. I was hoping you would join me. I have already told the guards you sent not to let anyone in the room and I left Ruana's lady's maid with her."

"Of course, I will join you in questioning the men," Loic said.

They reached the door to the dungeon and Proster stopped before reaching for the handle.

"What is it?" Loic asked.

"Nothing," Proster answered and then opened the door. He went first and Loic followed. The door was closed behind them.

Seath sat there watching Hertha sleep. Dr. Kayson had said Hertha was fine, but it had taken Seath a while longer before he was sure the doctor was correct. With his worries placated for the moment, Seath's mind was going back over the evening and the likely thoughts of others.

He realized that as the leader of the group from Grankle he was responsible for the actions of the two guards the king had sent with him. Seath had not bothered to keep track of the guards while they were here because he had not wanted to spent too much time around them himself. He had not thought to assign anyone else to do the job. There was also figuring that the guards would not have been let to roam the castle by Proster's men. Apparently he had been wrong to ignore them and now everyone from Grankle was likely suspect, including himself.

Seath without thinking got up and started pacing. Would Proster allow him to marry Hertha after the incident? Would he demand Seath pack up and leave immediately? Seath would not blame him if he did. After all, if someone had come on to his family estate and ignored people they were responsible for to the point of endangering his family, Seath would do the same thing.

But if Proster did kick him out, what would happen to Hertha? Would she have to find someone else to offer marriage? Would she have to go into hiding to prevent a scandal? Keften might have gotten her pregnant, but even if he found out about the child he was never going to be a father. Would Hertha find someone who could take the role? Seath had found himself once again in the position of caring for someone he might lose. At least this time, she would not be dead, just out of his reach. But what could he do about it all? Proster could tell him to go at any time.

Seath glanced around the room as if hoping the answer would be there. It did not seem to be. It was just a bedroom with the usual furnishings, unlike the guest suites which had several rooms all together. There would be paper in the guest suite; on the desk beside the pile of books he was reading. He could use the paper to write Proster a note explaining and apologizing for what happened. That would be what he could do to help. But the paper was in the guest room and he could not ask the guards outside to send a message to anyone to bring him some paper. The only person in his guest suite was likely to be Keften, if he made it back from whichever bed he should not be in. And Keften was the last person, Seath wanted to bring him paper to Hertha's room in the middle of the night. That was even if the guards were willing to send a message for him instead of kicking him out. Seath had heard Loic's instructions when the guards were changed to not let anyone in.

Seath looked around the room again. Hertha must keep some paper in her room. She did not have a writing desk, which was the most likely place to find paper, but he did see a shelf of books and what looked to be a pile of papers with them. Seath went over and looked at what was on the shelf. There was indeed a pile of papers there. He took the pile out. The first few had some writing on them, but the rest were blank. There was also a quill and ink pot. He put the papers with writing back on the shelf without reading them. Then he sat back down in the chair with the writing material and started his letter to Proster.

Seath was just about finished when Hertha rolled over and blinked at him. It took her a few minutes before she really woke up. She sat up and looked around.

"I had a really strange dream," Hertha said, "I dreamt the guards from Grankle had come in here and tried to kidnap me."

"It was not a dream," Seath said, "They knocked you out using an herb extract and tried to take you and your mother away. Darwin alerted your father. I happened to be going for a walk at the time and was able to help stop it from happening."

"Why?" Hertha said. She had gone a little pale and lay back down. She turned on her side so she could look at him.

"I do not really know," Seath answered, "They were doing it on the King of Grankle's orders, but what he expected to get out of kidnapping you, I do not know."

"What is that?" Hertha asked pointing to the paper.

"A letter to your father," Seath said, "I thought I might explain my side of the whole attempted kidnapping and disassociate myself from it."

"I doubt he believes you had anything to do with it," Hertha said, "Especially if you helped stop it."

"I just want to make sure he knows where I stand on the whole thing," Seath said.

"If it helps you," Hertha said. She yawned.

"Rest," Seath said, "No one else is going to bother you tonight and you need your sleep."

"I will try," Hertha said. She closed her eyes. In minutes, Hertha was back asleep. Seath pulled the blanket up to her shoulder before going back to the letter.

The sun was shining in the window when there came a knock at the door. Seath jerked awake and looked around. Hertha was still asleep and no one else was in the room. Everything looked exactly as it had been when he had drifted off the sleep.

The knock came again and Seath went to the door. He opened it to find Proster and Loic standing there with the guards standing to each side. Loic did not look happy to see him.

"We need to speak with you for a moment," Proster waved for Seath to step out of the room. Seath did so and closed the door most of the way behind him.

"What did you learn?" Seath asked.

"The King of Grankle was planning on holding Ruana and Hertha for ransom," Proster answered, "In hopes they could be traded for the resources Grankle needs."

"Grankle does not need the resources badly enough

to kidnap anyone," Seath said.

"That was the reason the guards gave for their actions," Proster replied, "And I believe them. It might not be there real reason, but the one the King of Grankle told them to get them to go through with his plan. However, I cannot think of any reason the King of Grankle would have personal issues with my family."

"I have heard nothing that would suggest any personal issues," Seath said, "Since Alaric took the throne it has been hard to tell exactly what is going on."

"Alaric never seemed like that smart a person, or this scheming," Loic said, "I thought he was more likely to spend his time claiming everyone should desire peace."

"The problem with Alaric is that he is not strong enough to rule on his own," Proster said, "He is being told his kingdom needs resources to survive, so he keeps looking for ways to get them. He has been getting ideas from the noblemen interested in power, who are giving him advice. He might have seen kidnapping as a peaceful way to gain resources since every trade agreement has gone back to Grankle unsigned.

"It is only a matter time before the noblemen figure out they do not need Alaric. It may be sooner after this scheme does not work. They will decide to do something about him, but the issue will be who gets the power once he is gone."

"Then we may be in more danger," Loic said.

"With the hunger for power in the capital?" Seath said, "I doubt it. The stories of them are known all over Grankle. It will take them a while to figure out who gets what position because everyone will want the most power and given everyone else the least."

"We need to deal with the current issue," Proster

said, "Anything that happens to Alaric is truly his own fault. We need to question the rest of your party as to whether or not they knew about the kidnapping attempt."

"You have my permission to do so," Seath said, "And if any of them refuse, send for me. I will let them know their options."

"Good," Proster said, "We want as few issues as possible with this."

"I wrote out my own statement," Seath said.

"Have the castle steward put it on my desk when he delivers the meals," Proster said, "He should deliver one to Hertha as soon as breakfast is ready, since he has orders to do so."

"I will do that," Seath said.

"I have called a meeting in the throne room for tomorrow morning," Proster said, "I should be finished questioning your people by then and have all the answers I am looking for. I have already sent word about the meeting to others. I expect both you and Hertha to be there."

"Okay," Seath nodded. He went back into the room while Proster and Loic headed down the hallway. Seath closed the door behind him and heard the guards move back in front of the door. He went back to the chair and sat down. Hertha was still sleeping. After a few minutes, Seath flipped to the next piece of paper and started writing the message he was going to send to the King of Grankle.

Proster stared at the pile of papers sitting on his desk. He had finished questioning all of the people from Grankle last night and he had managed to get a full night's sleep. Now, he was staring at the paper work left for him by Herwin and Garrick from the lower court. Apparently they had not heard about the kidnapping attempt or they had decided he still needed to pay attention to what was going on in his kingdom. Either way, he was not ready to deal with the paperwork.

There would be time to deal with it later and he very much intended to get help dealing with it. Herwin and Garrick could not complain about his lack of commitment to his kingdom if he was teaching his heir about running the kingdom. And Zebulon needed to learn these things anyway. Zebulon was supposed to be at the meeting with everyone else and Proster would talk to him about it then.

A knock came at the door.

"Come in," Proster called.

The door opened and Loic stepped inside. He closed the door behind him before facing Proster.

"Everyone is waiting in the throne room for you," Loic said.

"Yes, I was just getting there," Proster said as he remained seated. Loic did not appear to expect him to move.

"Thane told me about your attacks," Loic said, "It explains much of your behaviour lately."

"And?" Proster asked.

"I brought you the notes I took while we were questioning Lord Pardes' people," Loic took out the pieces of parchment and set them on Proster's desk, "In case you need to reference them. Should you need any help, please be willing to ask for it."

"I will," Proster said as he took the notes. He

glanced at them briefly before getting to his feet. He remembered all the information today. Proster went through the papers he had set to one side of his desk. He found the ones he wanted.

"Let us go get this done with," Proster said taking the papers with him as he headed to the door which would take them straight into the throne room.

"Yes, sire," Loic said following him.

Proster opened the door and they stepped into the throne room. He walked to the dais and went to the throne. He sat down and looked over the room. Lord Pardes was standing with his group on one side of the room, Herwin and Garrick was a few other noblemen were in the middle, and Ruana stood with their children on the other side of the throne room. Loic took up his position behind Proster.

"As most of you know, there has been an incident," Proster said, "The incident is why you all are standing here. The two guards from Grankle decided to go with their king's plan to abduct two members of the Proster royal family and are now spending their time in the dungeon. They will be removed in the next few days and transported to a slave mine nearby to complete their sentence. From here on, I consider any further attempts against the royal family of Proster an act of war."

Lord Pardes nodded, but did not say anything.

"After questioning the rest of the group from Grankle, I have determined none of them knew about the planned abduction," Proster said, "So, the rest are not being held. Lord Pardes, I understand you are prepared to send a messenger back to Grankle."

"Yes, Your Majesty," Lord Pardes replied.

"Good," Proster said, "Perhaps you can include this

and send the messenger off." Proster held out a piece of paper. Loic took it and walked it over to Lord Pardes.

"Of course, Your Majesty," Lord Pardes said with a bow. He handed the paper to Keften along with several others before giving Keften some instructions in a volume too low for most of the rest of the court to hear. Keften then nodded to Lord Pardes, bowed to Proster, and hurried out of the room. Proster waited until Keften was gone before speaking again.

"The King of Grankle is not likely to appreciate my letter," Proster said, "I hope you are not upset if he imprisons your assistant or something worse."

"Keften was nearing the end of his service anyway," Lord Pardes replied, "If the King of Grankle lets him free, he will be returning to his wife in the capital and his previous job."

"Excellent," Proster said, "That is all I have to say on the subject of Grankle for now. I ask that Lord Pardes stay, but the rest can go." The group checked with Lord Pardes, who nodded, before they shuffled out of the throne room.

"The next thing I bring to your attention is a matter of succession," Proster said, "I have been told I should name my successor and so I will. My son, Zebulon, is to rein when I am gone and as such shall begin his education in the role starting this afternoon."

Zebulon looked surprised by the contents rather than the announcement. Everyone else just nodded. Herwin and Garrick looked like they were waiting for him to dismiss everyone, but the rest of them stood waiting for any other announcements.

"And the final thing I wish to address is the request from Lord Pardes," Proster said. Herwin and Garrick glanced at each other and got ready to object to anything bad for the kingdom. Lord Pardes stepped forward.

"You asked for my daughter's hand in marriage," Proster said, "And after careful thought I have decided to grant you this request."

"Thank you, Your Majesty," Lord Pardes said with a smile and a bow. He looked relieved. Hertha also gave a smile of genuine happiness, which made Proster feel better about his decision.

"Everyone is dismissed," Proster said. Lord Pardes and Hertha went out together with Zebulon following them. Herwin and Garrick left a little confused as to what was going on with Loic ushering them out. But Ruana stayed where she was until after everyone was out and the door was closed.

Proster relaxed and sighed in relief. Ruana came up on the dais and took Proster's hand.

"There will be more questions later," Ruana said, "When I leave after the wedding. Zebulon will have more questions."

"I know," Proster said, "But he is not likely to have time for questions once I set him to work dealing with the cases Herwin and Garrick have been sending from the lower court. And then the only one who will miss you is me."

"I will miss you too," Ruana said, "I think my next few days will be busy since I have to pack as well as help plan a wedding."

"You can ask them if they want to use the castle chapel," Proster said.

"Castle chapel?" Ruana asked, "Where is it?"

"It is the stain glass windows on the shorter tower,"

Proster answered, "You are going to have to get the steward to hire some cleaners, but it should be big enough to accommodate everyone who should be invited."

"I have lived in this castle for a long time and I still do not know everything here," Ruana said, "I will talk to the steward after I have had a look at the chapel. I need to talk to Hertha about what she wants, so I might as well take her up there with me. But you need to rest. One night sleep does not make up for missing some, especially with your condition."

"I will," Proster said. He kissed Ruana's hand and then let it go. She kissed his forehead and then left the throne room. Proster went into this office and laid down on the couch to get a nap before lunch.

Hertha decided she wanted to get married in the chapel after she and Ruana viewed it. Ruana arranged to have the castle chapel cleaned for the ceremony. She also had the decorator come and get it ready. Lord Pardes and Hertha set a date for the next week and the preparations got underway. A dress was made quickly and only those close to the bride and groom were invited to attend.

The priest from the city church was requested to perform the ceremony. The meat for wedding feast would be put on by the man who ran the stall in the market place Hertha and Darwin enjoyed so much. The castle kitchens put together the rest of the feast. All other preparations were dealt with.

The day arrived and everyone knew where they were supposed to be. Hertha was isolated for the morning as her maid and her mother helped her get ready. When it was close to time, Hertha was led to the small room outside the door to the castle chapel. Her maid waited with her, but Ruana had to find her seat.

It was shortly before everything would begin there came a knock at the door. The maid opened it and after seeing who it was let Proster inside. Proster smiled at Hertha when he saw her.

"You are beautiful," Proster said.

"Thank you," Hertha said.

"Are you ready?" Proster asked.

"I think so," Hertha replied.

"It will be all right," Proster said taking his daughter's hand and giving it a squeeze. She smiled at him.

"Come," Proster said, "Let us see if we can find your happily ever after." Proster led Hertha out of the room and to the door of the chapel, which were closed with the two ushers waiting to open them and reveal the bride. Hertha took a deep breath when the wedding march started. Proster waited until she nodded before signalling the ushers to open the doors.

Proster walked his daughter down the aisle and handed her off to Lord Seath Pardes of Grankle. And once both were before him, the priest started:

"God, for the joy of this occasion, we thank you. For the significance of this wedding day, we thank you. For this important moment in an ever growing relationship, we thank you. For your presence here and now and for your presence at all times, we thank you. In God's holy name. Amen."

"Let me charge you both to remember, that your future happiness is to be found in mutual consideration, patience, kindness, confidence, and affection. Lord Seath Pardes of Grankle, it is your duty to love Princess Hertha of Proster as yourself, provide tender leadership, and protect her from danger. Princess Hertha of Proster, it is your duty to treat Lord Seath Pardes of Grankle with respect, support him, and create a healthy, happy home. It is the duty of each of you to find the greatest joy in the company of the other; to remember that in both interest and affection, you are to be one and undivided."

"Lord Seath Pardes of Grankle and Princess Hertha of Proster, you have made a very serious and important decision in choosing to marry each other today. You are entering into a sacred covenant as life partners in God. The quality of your marriage will reflect what you put into nurturing this relationship. You have the opportunity to go forward from this day to create a faithful, kind, and tender relationship. We bless you this day. It is up to you to keep the blessings flowing each and every day of your lives together. We wish for you the wisdom, compassion, and constancy to create a peaceful sanctuary in which you can both grow in love.

"Lord Seath Pardes of Grankle, do you understand and accept this responsibility, and do you promise to do your very best each day to create a loving, healthy, and happy marriage?"

"Yes, I do," Lord Pardes answered.

"Princess Hertha of Proster, do you understand and accept this responsibility, and do you promise to do your very best each day to create a loving, healthy, and happy marriage?"

"Yes, I do." Hertha answered.

"I, Lord Seath Pardes of Grankle, take you Princess

Hertha of Proster, to be my wedded wife, to have and to hold from this day forward, for better for worse, for richer or for poorer, in sickness and in health, to love and to cherish, 'til death do us part: according to God's holy ordinance, and thereto I pledge you my love and faithfulness," Lord Pardes said as he slipped the ring that had been handed to him on to Hertha's finger.

"I, Princess Hertha of Proster, take you Lord Seath Pardes of Grankle, to be my wedded husband, to have and to hold from this day forward, for better for worse, for richer or for poorer, in sickness and in health, to love and to cherish, 'til death do us part: according to God's holy ordinance, and thereto I pledge you my love and faithfulness," Hertha said as she put the ring on Lord Pardes' finger.

Lord Pardes and Hertha each took a candle from the stand. The priest started again:

"The two outside candles have been lighted to represent both your lives in this moment. They are two distinct lights, each capable of going their separate ways. As you join now in marriage, there is a merging of these two lights into one light. This is what God meant when He said, 'On this account a man shall leave his father and mother and be joined to his wife and the two shall be one flesh.' From now on your thoughts shall be for each other rather than your individual selves. Your plans shall be mutual, your joys and sorrows shall be shared alike. As you each take a candle and together light the center one, you will extinguish your own candles, thus letting the center candle represent the union of your lives into one flesh. As this one light cannot be divided, neither shall your lives be divided but a united testimony in a Godly home. May the radiance of this one light be a testimony of your unity in God."

Lord Pardes and Hertha lit the single candle before putting the two back in their places.

"Because Lord Seath Pardes of Grankle and Princess Hertha of Proster have desired each other in marriage, and have witnessed this before God and our gathering, affirming their acceptance of the responsibilities of such a union, and have pledged their love and faith to each other, sealing their vows in the giving and receiving of rings, I do proclaim that they are husband and wife in the sight of God and man. Let all people here and everywhere recognize and respect this holy union, now and forever," the priest said, "May the love of God be above you to overshadow you, beneath you to uphold you, before you to guide you, behind you to protect you, close beside you and within you to make you able for all things, and to reward your faithfulness with the joy and peace which the world cannot give, neither can it take away. Through God to whom be glory now and evermore. Amen.

"You may kiss the bride."

Lord Pardes and Hertha kissed very briefly.

"I now present Lord and Lady Pardes," the priest announced. The couple turned to the crowd for the applause and then headed back down the aisle hand in hand.

They went directly to the dining hall and the feast started. Everyone in the castle was invited to enjoy the feast and those could did attend. It lasted for several hours. It was very early the next morning before Lord Pardes and Hertha were able to slip away to the suite Proster had given them to share.

A couple days later, Hertha had packed up her stuff and helped carry some of it to the wagon to be loaded on before going to find her horse. She found Darwin finishing up getting her horse ready for the trip.

"I could have done it," Hertha said.

"I know," Darwin said looking up at her with a grin, "But since I had to get my horse ready I figured I might as well get yours ready as well."

"Why are you..." Hertha started to ask.

"I am going with you and the rest of the group to Grankle, of course," Darwin said, "I have to keep you out of trouble."

"And?" Hertha asked.

"I fell in love with their cook," Darwin asked, "We bumped into each other one day and things sort of went from there. And since you were headed for Grankle, I was not going to be left behind."

"I hope she appreciates you as much as I do," Hertha said with a smiled. Darwin smiled back and then finished with Hertha's horse.

When everyone had gathered and all the baggage was stowed, Proster, Ruana, Zebulon came out to say good bye. A few of the servants did so as well. Hertha gave everyone a hug and then was helped on to her horse. She and Lord Pardes led the group out of the court yard.

Proster and Ruana did not stop waving until the group was out of sight. Zebulon and the rest had headed inside as soon as Hertha was out of sight. Once the group was out of sight, Ruana signalled for her maid to bring her cloak and baggage. Her maid brought her the cloak and baggage before hurrying to the stable to get the carriage.

"Are you sure you want me to leave?" Ruana asked Proster.

"I am sure," Proster answer, "I love you and I do not want you to see me die like this."

"But you will write until you can no longer do so?" Ruana asked.

"I put the reminder to do so at my desk where I will see it every day and remember to do so," Proster said.

The carriage pulled up near them and the driver got down. He loaded Ruana's baggage and then held the door for her.

"I love you," Ruana said.

"I love you too," Proster said before kissing her. He helped her into the carriage and let the driver close the door. The driver climbed back into his seat and got the horses moving.

Proster stood there watching his happily ever after leave until there was no sign of her and even then he continued to watch until Loic sent a guard to bring him in.

LETTER TO PROSTER

Proster was busy working at his desk in his study when there came a knock on the door. Proster thought it might be Zebulon asking about something he had seen in court this morning.

"Come in," Proster called without looking up. The door opened and the steward entered. Proster looked up at him in surprise.

"A messenger arrived with a letter for you," the steward said offering the envelope to Proster.

"Thank you," Proster said taking the envelope. The steward bowed and then left the study. Proster broke the seal on the letter and pulled out the slip of paper. He carefully unfolded it before starting to read it.

Dear Father and Mother,

I hope all is well for you and has been these past ten months. Seath and I have been doing well. The twins are healthy and happy. There is a boy, Antranig, and a girl, Kissa. They have everything they could want in this world, except maybe meeting their grandparents, the King and Queen of Proster. I have found myself already telling them some of your stories and hope they never grow out of them. I will try and send you a picture as soon as I can, but we have gotten very busy these last two weeks.

Seath has gotten his wish to go and study at the great library and I will be going along with the twins. The twins very much have a home at Seath's family estate, but I find myself uncomfortable at times. They treat me as if I am too valuable to do any work and as a princess their home is much too humble for me. They walk on tiptoes around me and I have asked them to stop referring to me as Princess Hertha and bowing. I do not know how other princesses deal with it, but it is highly annoying.

We have found a home big enough for us to move to while he is studying. We are taking a limited number of servants, mainly Darwin and his wife, Caralynn, who is currently due in two months. I am hoping in a house I can call my own, fewer people will refuse to let me take care of it. Seath is likely to be too busy either studying or spending time with the twins to worry about whether I act like a princess or not. Even now it does not bother him if I do work and when his mother complains about it he shrugs and asks why I should not do it.

The political climate here in Grankle is toxic and only your threat of war stopped the king from sending any more people to Proster. Seath has been asked for a report by the king, but when he did, the king refused to accept it as truth. So, Seath is now an unofficial enemy of the state, but he does not care. Once we are away *from Grankle, I do not believe we will go back. I do not know where we will end up, but it is unlikely to be Grankle or Proster.*

Seath said to thank you for the books you set with us. He had read all of them already and really wished he could have read some more from the castle library, but is pacified by the thought that the great library probably has copies of them. I appreciate the books of Hadden Grimes stories and hope the twins like them when they are old enough.

Word has reached us here that you will be stepping aside very soon and Zebulon will be crowned king in your place. It saddens me a little to hear the news, but I suppose you have your reasons. I know Zebulon will do his best at the job, but in my heart you are the king of Proster and the best that lived. I must get on with packing now. I will try to send a letter from our new home and perhaps a portrait of the twins if the time to paint it is found.

Your daughter, Hertha

Proster smiled as he refolded the letter. He tucked it back in the envelope, sealed the envelope, addressed it to Ruana, and then placed it in the pile meant for sending off. The steward would deal with it in the morning.

THE END OF THE TALE?

Mitchell put the book down on the table and looked at the fire. It seemed to close off the story of Proster's middle child, Hertha. If she never returned to the kingdom of Proster then it is unlikely she or her children will show up in another one of these books, which seem to be in order and telling the story of the royal family of this particular kingdom.

Mitchell got up and picked up the book. He placed the book back in the box, but did not immediately pick up the next one. Instead he went to the sideboard and poured himself a drink, which he set on the table beside the chair. He added another log to the fire before going back to the box. He picked up the next book and sat down in the chair. He got comfortable, took a sip of his drink, and then opened the book.

ABOUT THE AUTHOR

Heather Mantler is a lover of fairy tales and fables. She is also a student of psychology. She lives in Prince George, British Columbia and is a member of the writing group Scribblers Unanimous. Heather is always working on another story as she hopes to finish every story idea that she has ever written down. She was a nominee for the fiction category of the 2012 Prince George Regional Arts and Cultural Awards and short listed for the 2013 John Harris Fiction Awards. Heather encourages all her readers to post their reviews on Amazon or Good Reads.

www.ingramcontent.com/pod-product-compliance
Lightning Source LLC
Chambersburg PA
CBHW051513170626
46811CB00002B/797